blue

and other tales of obsessive love

blue

and other tales of obsessive love

Teji Grover

Translated from the Hindi by
Meena Arora Nayak

Vani Book Company
An imprint of Vani Prakashan Group

Vani Book Company

An imprint of Vani Prakashan Group

4695, 21-A, Daryaganj, New Delhi 110 002

Phone : +91 11 23273167 Fax : +91 11 23275710

India

Branches

Ashok Rajpath, Patna 800 004, Bihar

Coffee House Compus, Mahatma Gandhi Marg, Allahabad 211 001, Uttar Pradesh

Mahatma Gandhi International Hindi University, Wardha 442 001, Maharashtra

Motiya Park Opp. Water Tank, Sultania Road, Bhopal 462 001, Madhya Pradesh

Goripur Taliya Para, 313, R.B.C. Road 24- Parganas (North) Kolkata 743 166, West Bengal

Blue and Other Tales of Obsessive Love

by Teji Grover

Translated from the Hindi Original by Meena Arora Nayak

Neela and *Sapne Mein Prem Ki Saat Kahaniyan*

Published by Vani Prakashan (1999 & 2009)

ISBN : 978-81-948736-4-8

Fiction

First Edition: 2020

Printed on recycled paper

Price : ₹ 225

Printed at : Printwell, Focal Point, Amritsar

Vani Prakashan's signature motif is created by Artist Maqbool Fida Husain

Contents

To the memory of
Krishna Baldev Vaid,
Nirmal Verma and Ramchandra Gandhi

This Writing

Blue and Other Tales of Obsessive Love came into existence when I discovered that the short stories I had written much before the novel, *Blue* (*Neela* in Hindi) seemed in some way to anticipate the latter prose text, in which the white of the paper was so going to engage with color blue that all the subtle acts of love in the narrative were going to become even more congruent with acts of writing—to the extent that after a point, both these acts seemed to become too intimate to be separated even in the writing body that was overwhelmed by their desire to merge themselves. The writing body then wrote itself to a point where there seemed to be no way out of love, and, as a consequence, no way out of writing. It was a planet all its own—a planet on which all the flora and fauna were nothing but love, nothing but writing, and all was bathed in an intense blue that can only be produced by the erotic fusion of love with writing. Thus, blue became the tantalizing color of passion, of desire, and it was going to involve those readers who had a similar vulnerability to be seduced by blue. This writing itself was born from "transference," from acts of reading the texts of two women writers in particular: French writer Marguerite Duras, whose novels, *Lover* and *Blue Eyes Black Hair* and the Swedish writer Agneta Pleijel, whose novel, *The Dog Star (Hundstjärnan* in the original) were going to hurl me into what Paul Valery calls the "rare rectangle." But before this transference sent me like an arrow shot from Cupid's bow into this rectangle, I happened to visit Ingmar Bergman's land of rustling pines reflected in the still waters of those lakes we had glimpsed only in films before. Fellow Indian writers who were traveling with me were stung, like me, by those lakes and by the luminous russet-yellow splendor of the Swedish autumn. It was the beginning of a bouquet of love stories for some of us. One legendary Malayalam poet amongst us even swore he was endlessly seeing the face of his childhood sweetheart, trying to draw aside the yellow-red curtain of maple leaves to greet her lover in a foreign land. This is the space a writer wishes to inhabit, but this is the space she can seldom enter with the body heat that went into the writing of these texts that you're looking at now. As autumn advanced in that enchanted land, we were soon engulfed by darkness, during what was normally day for the sun-kissed poets we all had been and our biological clocks were broken beyond repair. *Blue*, or the writing of *Blue*, became the space where this clock was going to altogether step out of time into a dark and, sometimes, an ultramarine blue world that could not tell one thing apart from another. As the Polish Hindi scholar, Kamila Junik, who has worked extensively on my fiction and poetry, observed about *Blue* in one of her papers, "...The contours of the world and of the self become unclear."

With this inky autumnal blur that I was enfolded in, I became obsessed with the question: what language will I ever find for this blue that was nibbling at me? The question haunted me when I was back home where day gave me light and night brought me darkness. There was no dark blanket thrown over my being at an odd afternoon hour. But I had been unraveled by the autumn I had lived through in a distant land inhabited by the magician Ingmar Bergman. I don't really know if I ever found the language worthy of *Blue*, but what I did find is what I bring to this space I find for it. (But beware! My friend, the fiction writer, Meena Arora Nayak has already turned *Neela* into *Blue* and this she did touched by the same transference I had been touched by. More stories of transference will follow below.) Or maybe I should write down the two other titles *Blue* acquired by way of translation in the course of the transference we have noted. The translation in both cases, like in the English *Blue,* was experienced as writing. *Neela* became *Blękit* in Polish and ਨੀਲਾ in Panjabi. Meena, Bipanpreet, Kamila—the translators of *Blue,* are writers themselves, and all of them women.

The stories that formed part of a collection called *Seven Stories of Love in Dream (Sapne me Prem ki Saat Kahaniyan* in Hindi) were written much before the novel *Blue* came into existence. But looking back at the years during which they were written, I was able to observe the thread that connects them to the longer text, which was published as a novel (*Neela*) in Hindi in 1999. The first of these is the story of a nun ("Bhikshuni" in the original) who comes back from an unspecified realm to tell a barber a mesmerizing story of love and loss, in which she herself seems to have been a character in another unspecified life or epoch. The event of a cataclysmic cyclone predicted by the nun intertwines with a love affair that comprises of day and nightlong story-telling by the barber and his beloved to the child she has birthed. There's but one little chink in time when the lovers are able to make love, like novices, each time as if for the first and the last time in their lives. The last story in the present collection is called "Suparna" in Hindi, and "Suparna and I" in the English translation.

The younger of the two women in the story, is making an attempt to revive the older one's memory through elaborate rituals of intimacy that are punctuated by the wailing sounds of the older woman's mother, who is shocked by the nakedness of the rituals between the two women. Memories of the excessively tired older woman are supposed to drift through images in the mirror that's hanging on the glass wall of the house.

As I said earlier, all the stories accompanying the novel *Blue* have the same intertextual logic and are born of the same body heat; they are also linked together by the same incestuous union of the desire to write and the desire for love. The first story titled, "Bhikshuni" in the present collection, like its fellow texts in the collection of seven stories in Hindi, is told the way Indian texts of Upanishadic origin are told, by couching dream within dream, story within story, to achieve a state in which dream and reality are hard to tell apart. And this happens with walls of time that have been rendered porous and utterly transparent, as well. Studded with allusions from contemporary literature, the seven narratives dip into the lives of poets like Ted Hughes, Syliva Plath, Marina Tsvetayeva and two men Hindi poets I won't name here. But it is also contemporary events, like the 1984 tragedy of the gas leak in Bhopal, that surface time and again in these texts—disasters uprooting life on earth in a mythological framework, but, somehow, all held together within the larger frames of stories of love and obsessive desire. Though the blueness of love is the primary taste, there is also the terror when Bhopal and blue collide, stealing away an erotic space that then struggles to find its tender feet in an all too fragile world. But not only have the Upanishadic and Pauranic touched these stories with their narratorial strategies, but also the stories owe their existence to the films of Andrei Tarkovsky and to that other master who will loop the utterly contemporary and seemingly real, with fantasy, dream and political comment—Luis Bunuel.

I won't provide notes for the allusions to other literary texts and to contemporary events. In particular, any reader who researches, for instance, the Udayan-Vasavadutta story will find the search rewarding. This is true of other allusions and references. Also, I would like to keep the filmmaker, Ingmar, in the *Blue* text without his second name; you will see why….Then there is Bhopal present in the text, with its multiple meanings, touching the year 1984, when so much more was unleashed elsewhere in my country. Inevitably, Bhopal lurks in the texts of many writers as the alluring hub of intertextual writing and art.

But I am not quite done yet inserting my voice before these stories. Let me thank Renata Czekalska and her pupil, the Polish-Hindi scholar Kamila Junik for taking *Blue* on another trip, which not only involved a translation of *Neela* into Polish but also prompted her into doing a doctoral thesis on this tiny book, *Blue,* after she had translated it into Polish. She, apparently, played the academic, almost as if she were herself writing her own fiction in response to *Blue*. Her thesis turned into another book published in 2015, in which she placed *Blue* at the heart of a study about contemporary Hindi experimental prose: [*Literature as a process of writing. Analysis of Teji Grover's Nila (Blue) in the context of changes in contemporary Hindi prose*]. Kamila Junik, like her teacher Renata Czekalska, probed the nooks and crannies of *Blue* also by paying very close attention to my poetry and writing about the "transgressive imagination" she found in there.

I quote here some of Kamila's observations that she made in the course of her writing about *Blue,* just to remind myself of the two-way transference taking place between her texts and mine:

> *The moments of separation with the beloved make her weep for him, long for him in despair. Psychoanalysts*

Kakar and Ross compare such mad love with hunger, with pain, which are difficult to extinguish...

Writing predominates everywhere in the narrative. All the characters write. All the events are being written. Existence is being written as well. There is no other world beyond writing. Hence Blue *is the inner eye, the desire to write...*

When, at the sea, Blue *writes the narrator's name on the sand and lays her in that place, he symbolically calls her into existence, fragile and unstable, lasting only until the next tide.*

— Teji Grover

Bhikshuni*

There is a knock at my door. I open it. My room is drenched in the fragrance of tamarind. Outside there is a woman without any clothes on. Silver bells are braided in her long, curly tresses and a tiny, black silver foot is tied around her neck—a silver footprint in the dusky complexion of skin. I'm watching and I'm afraid.

Pushing me aside, she enters the room. Now she's sitting on the bed. Her legs dangling.

I sit on the floor close to her. She passes a smile. Her teeth have the whiteness of tamarind stones. She places a finger on her left breast and says, "S-a-m-b-a-r-i."** I, too, place a finger on my left breast and attempt to utter my name. But I'm unable to form the syllables. That mob of seventeen hundred names by which Babu used to address me, converges: Ninka, Janu, Babushi, Bubna, Jokhim…

Now it's her turn again. "No use," she says. "None of these names belong to you. Your inner substance is

* A woman who has renounced the world. ** Magic woman.

not addressed by any of these names. You are a perilous woman built in quick silver. Whenever you appear in trouble in another's dream, that other who is dreaming of you is in deep trouble."

I get up and sit on the bed beside her. Full of longing. Drawing her hair aside, I begin to suck on her left breast. My mouth is overflowing with salt water. I try to swallow. My belly begins to bloat.

"What you are drinking," she says, "is the water from the cyclone intended for the village of Edusmundi on the bank of Krishna River.

"There are fourteen mud-houses in that village which are being washed away by the storm. Except for one woman in the village, everyone else has, somehow, made it to dry land. That woman is squatting in labor and the water has risen to her lower lip."

Turning toward me, Sambari squeezes my left breast and spits in my eye. "Now the accounts between him and you are closed—he in whose eyes you once spat," she says. She raises my finger and, placing it on my left breast, says my name—"I-m-p-o-s-t-e-r."

"The man whose wife is birthing a child in the storm

is sitting atop the coconut tree. He sees no water. He sees no storm."

Evading Sambari's glance, I want to flee from this tale of hers. Her tresses fly and noose around my neck. I'm pulled onto her thigh. From there I'm listening, as if in a spell, to the following story...

A hundred years ago, a Bhikshuni arrived in the village of Edusmundi. The first thing she did was to go to the barber's house and have her head shaved. Cleaning his razor, as the barber made to get up, the Bhikshuni asked for a drink of water. Looking at her belly, the barber said, "In my house, there's water for you perhaps, but not for your child. This is no ordinary conception."

The Bhikshuni said, "Give me whatever water you have in your pitcher."

The barber got up and removed the lid from the pitcher. It was filled with white tamarind stones.

The barber said, "We are poor people. Why have you come to our village to dupe us in this way—in this disguise?"

"I didn't come," replied the Bhikshuni. Placing a hand on her stomach, she continued, "I'm walking the path suggested by this child. I have no path; I'm no one, because you can't tell who I am."

The barber picked up the pitcher and placed it before her. The Bhikshuni removed the lid and lowered her hand into the pitcher. The barber looked carefully at her copper ring. The stone set in it looked like a drop of water.

The Bhikshuni lifted out the tamarind stones from the pitcher with the ring hand and, squeezing them, began to drink the water of tamarind stones.

The barber saw that the Bhikshuni's transparent throat was of a light blue color down which the water trickled like a silver thread into her body.

In this way she drank seven fistfuls of tamarind stone water. Then, flinging the ring into the pitcher, she said, "Keep this ring. This ring belongs to your second wife."

"I don't even have a first wife yet," the barber replied smiling.

"I, too, have heard that some mortals seeing her don't

see her, even if she is sitting right before them, telling them a tale," said the Bhikshuni. "But listen to this carefully. After the cyclone, when Edusmundi emerges dry, begin to build your hut from this very spot where I'm placing this pitcher just now. No storm will be able to wash it away from here—

"When you return to your village after the waters recede, you'll hear an infant crying. Raising your hand and touching all along the sound of the voice, you'll reach him.

"Holding the infant, go stand at the riverbank until you see the water birds flying in from the east. That same moment turn around and you'll see a woman sitting on the ground. She'll have a deep wound in her head that'll be dripping onto her clothes.

"Sit beside her with the child. She'll ask you if you have seen the man who in his dream smashed her head against the wall. This question will remind you of one of your bad deeds. To make amends you should step forward and ask for her hand humbly and with utmost compassion. Then both of you should head slowly towards this spot. Look at this—the site of this pitcher, removing which you have to begin making your hut."

The barber asked, "There'll be a cyclone in Edusmundi... When will the storm come to pass?"

The Bhikshuni said, "This I can't tell you, but hear this about the child.

"This child will eat very little and will drink nothing. But the urge for story that all children of the earth experience together will turn into his urge. Anywhere on earth if a child is not being told the story that is essential for his survival, his tears will enter this child. That woman will not be able to carry out any other tasks, because she'll have to keep telling the child a story in which there are seeds, flowers, and fruits of never ending stories—a story that sounds as if it ends and begins at the same time, that which gives the ascending traveler the feeling of descent and the descending traveler a feeling of ascent..."

The barber asked fearfully, "—and at night?" The Bhikshuni said, "Of course, this child is wise enough to let the storyteller fall peacefully asleep at night, but now that you have interrupted me, it will not be so. At night you'll take the woman's place.

"This child will fall asleep only when, exhausted by

the night, you'll find this woman opening her eyes for the day. Longing for sleep, you'll find her so enticing that you'll desire her. The reason for the child's sleep is evident: story and love can in no way take place simultaneously, not even in a love story. While telling a story the awakening of love and desire is an illusion, a chimera. The desire is the desire only for the story, the love only love for the story.

"Similarly, every morning, you'll make love like two novices, as though you are meeting each other for the first and last time."

The barber began to tremble in fear. The curse of always having to tell a story—on him and his wife!

"Constantly telling stories, both of you will sometimes wish for deliverance—you'll wish to die to be released from this child. At this time meekly request the spirits that frequent your house to keep the child calm for a while. The spirits within the stories will continue the story exactly from where you tried to leave it, but weren't able to.

"That day of the month when the moon intoxicated tide rises, stay awake. Stand on the riverbank with your wife and child. That day that very same tide will take your place and calm the child. And you two will discover that that silence of yours which had been washed away, is flowing in your blood again. Before you curse your fate, just know that all the stories of the universe are born because each infant emerges from the womb with a thirst for story… If someone, without interrupting, witnesses from afar a child listening to a story, she's actually witnessing the very significance of the created world."

The barber asked, "But, that woman, my second wife?" "That woman is not your second wife," the Bhikshuni answered. "She has only come to you to break the fate of your second wife. She'll leave with *her* fate, and then you'll be able to live happily with that third woman. If this third woman had come instead of the second, she'd have drowned in the River Krishna on the seventh day of the wedding."

The barber grew distressed and asked, "But what…*what* will happen to her?"

The Bhikshuni thought for a while before saying, "One day the child will not want to hear the story she is spinning. For the first time she'll lift the jute curtain and look out. At that moment, take out the copper ring with the water-droplet stone from this pitcher and give it back to her.

"She'll not know when she lost this ring. Neither will she know that she's carrying a child.

"On seeing the ring, she'll want to cling to you and weep. She'll get only one message from that ring—that you don't love her and you wish her to leave your hut.

"She'll show you the wound on her head and say that the wound you have given her has not healed yet, that as soon as it heals she'll leave on her own, without uttering another word.

"She'll say that stories are overflowing in her like a river of milk. That she can't do without the child living in that hut.

"No matter how filled with compassion you feel, don't utter a word. She'll read your silence in as many ways as the stories she has told.

"She'll reflect upon each meaning and, shredding it to pieces, she'll weep. She'll weep inconsolably. And then suddenly she'll calm down and say, 'Don't look at these tears, don't look—'

"She'll rise and, drawing the jute curtain aside—"

The barber asked in deep distress, "But how is it...how is it that I'll let her leave like this...?"

"You interrupt a great deal. And with each interruption your fate grows fickle. But because you are interrupting from being deeply immersed in the story, I'm holding your fate securely. You'll let her go because in that hour of separation, Shiva's snake garland will be shedding its skin. In this hour no one can stop departing beloveds from leaving.

"Unaware of the fact that she's carrying a child, she'll start walking towards River Krishna.

"Standing at the threshold, you'll watch her leave, because one of the purposes of your being in this world is to helplessly watch your loved ones leave.

"Your eyes will fill with tears we can't shed while telling a story."

As the Bhikshuni said this, she pretended to pick something from the floor, so the barber wouldn't see her face.

When the Bhikshuni looked at the barber again, he couldn't recognize those eyes in which, until moments ago, there were no signs of this-worldliness.

"When the storm waters recede from Edusmundi, please give this message to the people of those fourteen crumbled houses: that images from the past change each time you try and recall them. It's not possible to preserve even a dream as it is. Whatever changes when we recreate memory and dream, fate changes in exactly the same way, in that very same direction. That's why in a way the creation of fate is not altogether devoid of human endeavor."

The barber wanted to know when some calamity befalls a million people, animals, birds and plants together at the same time, like a cyclone for instance, then whose recreation of memory and whose recreation of dream makes it their fate—

But where was the Bhikshuni to be seen by then!

My Poet

A woman is sitting in the train across from me. Her name begins with 'O'. She has light brown, sparkling eyes. When I look at her carefully, I recognize the distinctive traits of her face. She is my poet's sister. My heart begins to pound. 'O' is wearing a tight, beige skirt, and the flamboyance of her shoes is beyond my comprehension.

I should grab her shoulders and ask her, instantly, where is her brother. Can 'O' tell him that I am someone, and I've been dying to meet him for a long time?

With the blood still pounding in my heart, I start reading the newspaper.

On the last page, in a tiny corner, there's brief news. He's in India to meet a Lama in search of some Tibetan manuscript. I'm sure that it's a manuscript related to the *Book of the Dead*. A more ancient kernel of his poetry that I don't have.

Leaving 'O', I begin to walk down the aisles in the train, looking closely at each passenger.

There's sand swirling everywhere. The breeze is gentle, but the sand is ferociously adrift.

But, here's a pile that isn't moving. Someone is sitting beside it. The wind is against me, so is the sand; despite that, I reach him. He's making what appears to be a fort in the sand. All around it are narrow drains in which water, the color of blue, is flowing. One of his feet is buried in the sand. He pulls it out and, on the main gate of the fort, plants a tiny, watery flag.

With a child-like simplicity that sounds silly even to my own ears, I say, "I have every book of yours. I even have a copy of the manuscript that's in the British museum."

He smoothens the turret of the fort with one last pat. Then, turning his back towards me, he begins walking away quickly. His awareness that I'm behind him feels like a touch, and, once again, I am reminded. The last time he was invited to India, it was to straighten out the little finger of some infant-angel sculpted on the facade of a decaying church. When I arrived at the church, he wasn't there. The little finger had been straightened out.

Like an automated toy, I run behind him. I'm unable

to keep quiet. Why doesn't he know that he exists in me? Why doesn't he know that this is unbearable for me?

"The Lama that you have to meet, Babu is there—with him." I say to him. But how foolish I am. How would he know who Babu is?

He's not listening to anything. He doesn't even turn around. Is he too, dead—like Sylvia?

I am afraid. The poem about Sylvia's death wish is now like a waft of smoke between us: *Dying is an art like everything else.*

I want to ask, don't Frieda and Nicholas miss their mother? But I'm embarrassed at the absurdity of my questions.

I'm surprised that he's wearing a blue shirt; he doesn't like the color blue.

Walking along, we have come to my grandmother's house. Straight away, he turns towards that beautiful ruin that has the same locks it used to have in the past.

Children are playing gullidanda outside the mansion. I, too, am among them, wearing a frock with yellow roses. If it felt right, I would remain behind to meet my six-year-old look-alike. But this is not the time for meetings.

Without talking to the children, we unlock the chainlet of the brass door and enter the mansion.

The door opens; inside is a vast swamp. Next to the swamp, there is a narrow, circular staircase—a banister of circles loaded with vines and blooms of white iron. Above the stairs is a very delicate railing, almost like a trellis of water, and behind this watery railing is a big-sized balcony.

Everything has already been decided. The way we begin walking in the swamp, without any effort, like an innately choreographed dance.

He stops before a niche in the yellow mud wall and begins cleaning out the cobwebs.

I have to climb the iron staircase and go stand in the balcony. With this intention, I look towards him. His clothes are dissolving on his body, and the soft wave like creases that rise in them, slowly merge, becoming calm.

I have no patience. I want to tell him, immediately, about those dreams in which he often came for trout fishing in the dirty rivers of my country. I want to tell him that even after awakening, I continue to see this dream. He turns to look at me, as though asking me to be quiet.

I turn towards the iron staircase. On each stair lingers the fragrance of his dead wife—*any more black shoe in which I have lived like a foot for thirty years.* My clothes begin to get caught in the fine carvings of the banister. I remove them and throw them under the stairs.

I'm standing, leaning my arms on the railing. He's standing below in the swamp, holding a black-colored musical instrument. I have no idea what this instrument is. Sometimes he raises it to his lips and begins to play on it like a flute, and sometimes he strums it, till its strings resonate.

A faint tinkling of bells streams in from somewhere, and now the end notes of an unfamiliar raag played on the santoor disappear towards the horizon, exactly in the shape of a white dove.

Now he's dancing before the niche. His eyes are closed. And while he's dancing, his hair begins to grow longer.

I suddenly glance at the niche. Inside it, on its wall, statuettes of miniature white animals are slowly emerging.

At the very bottom is a cow, and the bell around her neck has rung. From between her legs, the head of calf is peeping out.

And now a deer…

And now a white elephant with tusks…

The bells are beginning to sound louder now. There's a sound of rain; then a flood. Thousands of animals pant in the water. Now a white sea-horse has emerged in the yellow niche.

And now a camel, who moves to the front and partly conceals the cow.

The niche keeps filling with these white miniatures, and I start panting desperately. What have I done that I should be here, before the niche, the lone witness of this scene? Whose share have I come to steal? My poet's dance, the tinkling of bells, the one-by-one evocation of white animal statuettes—surely all this is not for me!

Wearing a yellow outfit with a bouquet of roses, Sylvia is walking in from the main door.

The music has stopped. In the niche, a rabbit's second ear was forming; it ceases.

This is the first time that Sylvia is traveling after her death. Having searched for her husband for a long time, she has arrived here.

She's wearing the same frock as my double, playing outside the mansion. Seeing the bouquet of roses on yellow, I understand for the first time that the word, 'death' has no meaning.

She begins to move towards him. The embarrassment in her smile is exactly the same as mine. But what I am doing here between the two of them?

Then she touches him, as a wounded person touches someone after an accident.

Her husband's hair has grown to his waist. Sylvia steps forwards, and with her deft fingers, begins to tie-up his hair in very fine braids. He sits without moving, his head bowed, absorbing the delicateness of Sylvia's rituals. Then, she removes a pair of small hoop earrings from the pocket of her yellow frock and puts them in his ears.

Once again he lifts his black instrument. Again the

transparent sound of bells and the endnotes of an unfamiliar raag played on the santoor, disappearing into the horizon in the form of a white dove.

The dance has begun again. A small wave trembles, then a bigger one, and near the horizon, once again, a great moon-intoxicated swell.

The language in which Sylvia is expressing her thoughts is not mine.

I look towards the niche in the wall. A swan swimming in the sound of water has become still.

Fluttering her marble-clad wings, one fish has come to a standstill.

The ear of the rabbit that had stopped forming at Sylvia's arrival, begins to grow again. Sylvia dances her arms in the air in snake-like gestures. I try to hear her mantras very carefully. Can I not participate in her chanting?

My poet's braids have also started waving in the breeze—my magical dancer, like some tree full of leaves. Standing a moment in the shade of this tree, I can ask for anything.

But suddenly everything comes to a halt.

There's a word in Sylvia's mantra that she has forgotten. She glances at me, as though that word belongs exclusively to me.

I don't know that word. I don't know what I'm going to say, but still that word which Sylvia has forgotten slips out of my mouth. I don't know what this word means. As soon as Sylvia hears it, she lifts her arms towards me. There is affection in her smile, a celebration, and a comforting deep sadness.

My eyes begin to tear. I descend the stairs and once again join the dance. I don't know how to dance, yet, I'm dancing—the same rhythm as them, the same fluidity.

The chainlet on the brass door sounds. This must be my mother.

Those two stop their dance for my sake. I run towards the door, thoroughly embarrassed. Now my feet don't move with the same ease in the swamp.

I open the door. My mother is standing outside, wearing a garish orange-colored sari that reaches only down to her knees. I'm astonished to see her like this, because she always wears long-sleeved blouses, and the edge of her sari is always below her ankles. Her annoyed face reveals how tired she is from searching for me. I try to send her away. But my mother has more grit than I. Grabbing my arm, she comes inside the mansion.

I have lost the fluidity of the dance. The scene that I'm presenting has no beauty in it any more. In the meantime, they have started dancing without me. More animals are now emerging in the niche. And here I am, standing with my hand covering my mother's mouth.

Flinging my hand aside, she inspects the mansion and steps into the swamp. There's no way I can stop her. I remember that this is my maternal grandmother's mansion. Did my mother know about this swamp? Why has she tied her sari so high up? There is no choreography in her steps, yet she is holding her own in the swamp.

I, on the other hand, am not even able to walk like my mother. My footsteps squelching in the sinking mud, trying to talk to my mother, I reach there where they both are—now barely dancing. For me, everything is ruined. If my mother can barge into this place, as well, there is no reason for my life. I try one last time to deter her. Squeezing her affectionately, I say in her ear, "Please don't say anything Ammi. This is my poet and along with him..."

It suddenly dawns on me that I have no clothes on. Neither does my poet. And Sylvia's frock! How long will it take Ammi to figure out that this is same frock I'm wearing as I play gullidanda outside. She'll be so angry—why did I let a dead woman wear my clothes?

But mother doesn't say anything in this regard. Instead, in a loud voice, she announces, "Oh this is that very same poet on whom you are writing..."

I try to garner some patience that is greater than I am: "Ammu, can you please turn towards the wall and remain quiet for a little while? I know that when I open my eyes there won't be anything here."

I look towards them. He is near the niche; Sylvia is on the other side—both sweetly tired from the labor of the dance, its evidence present in the various motionless gestures of the miniature white animals in the niche.

No, I shouldn't have said to Ammi that in a little while when I open my eyes…

They are looking at me silently. The words that their gaze have evoked inside me are:

Will your eyes ever open any more than this?

Gray Flowers etc.

"Just shove him off some mountain! The unformed world inside him will get stirred into shape. Half his blood is white; half red. His left eye is of glass, and in the right, flimsy shadows of some alien earth go swinging by. There is no connection, not even through a vein, of the left eye's marble to the ghostly spirits of the right eye. In one of his lungs, a kite flutters, and in the other, a parrot of sand. At any given moment, it's one color that flows over him, and it's quite another one that recedes. Wind and water, fire, sky and earth lie within him untranslated, like different languages. Just shove him off some mountain! Everything will get stirred into shape. Then, on some alluring piece of earth, he could last for a long time. Dressed in a white shirt, if he tries, he could enjoy the taste of yogurt and beets at any spread. Without cutting his fingers, he could manage to slice apples, etc. He could well have the power to restore the laughter of children, butterflies, and colors. Just shove him off some mountain once!"

The prescription that this man has been given is yet to be tested. It isn't as if there are dividing lines etched in his heart, in his thoughts. It's just that he lacks blending; he hasn't been properly kneaded. Inside him, the towns of his childhood and youth are separately inhabited. In his heart, the beloved characters of all the novels he has read so far have not transformed into a unit from which passionate paradigms of living can be lifted. All those characters keep sprinkling their individual salts in his blood, from which smoke, and who knows what else, keeps rising from time to time. The satchels of his children are filled with erasers. This man doesn't buy his children a single colored pencil. The children just keep rubbing their erasers on the wall, making gray flowers, etc. Although his wife can't read or write, she is farsighted; but the man makes her wear glasses meant for nearsightedness. Every tree planted in his small garden emits the mean fragrance of green gourd—even the lemon blooms. In his town, neither is mulberry sold nor is black jamun. Nor does rain ever leave a marsh behind. In fact, in his new town, each drop of rain itself arranges a different path. In his new town, no one has ever heard a cat slip into a house to drink milk, and no one has ever seen a mongoose cross the road. Even then, a kite flutters in one of his lungs, although his town knows as much about kites as his marble eye knows about the eye with ghostly spirits.

Because of his insistence, his wife, perforce, wears glasses meant for nearsightedness, and before kissing his face, ends up kissing the table, chair, wall, etc., and sometimes even that wall, on which, in a particular light, the rubbed in gray flowers etc. begin to gleam. It's because of kissing these flowers that she is so close to her children. But he feels no jealousy about the closeness between his wife and children. Also, because this man only buys erasers for his children, and they make flowers etc. with those, it can't be said that he doesn't love the children. When this man disappears for a year without informing anyone, the children, instead of making flowers on the wall, make letter-to-a-father like flowers on paper. But the mother and children never have the address for the letters.

It's only his year-long, solitary journeys that simultaneously soothe his tattered, raggedly soul and his carefree, colored-kite housing lung. He's convinced that while he's engaged in reading and writing, music and dance, drama and pageantry, love and friendship, intensity of hatred and stories of struggle—only one can be touched, and if lung and soul both are touched, it can never be at the same time and never equally. In friendships outside the house, this man will often glow dark red, like the jujube fruit. In hatred, he unwittingly walks their walk, laughs their laugh, wears clothes like them and talks in the speech of those whom he so hates. And if he suddenly catches himself doing this, he becomes like that earthworm who has just had salt sprinkled on its back. When he watches some comedy show, he breathes only with his kite lung, and, after breathing one-sidedly for a while, he grows afraid that he'll get paralyzed on one side. When he returns to writing, his tattered soul scares all the birds into flight. If he wants to make love to his wife, he doesn't let her remove the glasses of nearsightedness; so the woman sees strange shapes of this man who has leapt on her. Like those vultures who, just a moment before tearing into their prey, shrink so much that they are able to eat only an antworth of meat. Opening her eyes forcibly, she tolerates all this only because, let alone a book, she hasn't read so much as a poem. She thinks that this is what she has to suffer for the rest of her life as pay back. As soon as this man discovers that his wife is simply enduring him, and her glasses have become foggy from her tears, he leaps out of the bed and, leaning his head on the wall, weeps copiously. And the mean fragrance of green gourd rising from the room is absorbed in the tatters of his soul.

Immediately after tragedies such as these, the man disappears from home for a whole year. Only the forest will touch him; or, the dazzle of snowy mountains, the poisonous water from the mix of ocean and snake; pythons, hanging like heavy branches from trees; boats with delicate white and sky blue sails. This is what will simultaneously touch the man's sad soul and kite lung—with equal pressure. During these journeys, not a single shadow of a thought crosses this man's mind that perhaps changing the glasses may do the trick. Or perhaps, colored pencils. But he's unwilling to accept that such deep spiritual and physical issues could have such simple solutions. If the prescription is too simplified, the patient could die of shame. Prescriptions should be like this: Just shove him off some mountain once!

During his journeys, although the children stop growing and blossoming, the wife can give her spinning head a rest by removing, or even changing, her glasses. She's able to kiss the children directly, and because, during this year, the gray flowers, etc. will be drawn in letters rather than on walls, there's no fear that instead of kissing the children, she'll end up kissing the wall. The children also stop growing and blossoming because they dream about mulberry and black jamun, and when they awaken in the morning, they exhaust themselves from demanding things whose names they don't even know. They were born in this very town in which mulberry and black jamun are unknown fruits. And they don't know that in the old town of his childhood, their father used to eat these fruits to his heart's content. The surprising thing is that when this man returns home after a year, his children are no longer plagued with dreams of mulberry and black jamun.

But sometime after returning home, this man starts saying—in a manner of—who knows which book—that I'm the one who stole fire from the gods and am now tied to this rock; look how vultures are clawing at me! Or that, at thirty, I should surely return His ticket to God. Then he gets irritated at himself. "Oh you parrot of sand," he says to himself, as though cussing in some highly complicated family invective. Living the life of characters from novels, he dies many times and ends up somewhere else, much like that man who, in search of water at night, leaves his body and slips into an uncovered water-pot but is unable to return to his body, because someone has covered the pot, with him in it.

Now, it isn't that this man can spend many more days counting on his straight-out-of-a-novel, sand-parrot lung.

This man begins remembering in some deep recesses of his mind that when he goes with his wife to visit his old town, where rain creates many marshes, where there aren't separate paths for each rain drop, people will tease him by calling him, 'his lordship'; that they will look at him as though he were the emperor of kites. And when, crossing rain swamps, he and his wife will enter his old house, people will remember those kites, damp from the rain, being laid out in the courtyard sun. That seeing him, women of the neighborhood will whisper: Look. It's he who brought home a bride by boasting that he plundered Bijli, the wrestler's kites many times—those kites that Bijli lost in flying contests and then handed out hundred rupee notes to anyone who plundered them and brought them back to him. This man's claim was that he had plundered hundreds of kites which flew from the wrestler's terrace and then had received many hundreds from him in return of the kites.

But now, listening to the gibes of the neighborhood women, this man doesn't know whether he'll relate the tales about hundred rupee prizes to his children or not—tales of hundred rupees in the days when the prize money for a bandit's head used to be just five rupees. Will this man ever be able to tell how the prize kite used to fly at such a blinding height that half the town's boys would get up while it was still dark and ride their bicycles in the direction of the wind for miles, till they reached the outlying villages. And the other half would ride, with lungs bursting, the same distance towards the villages, but in the opposite direction? Those who went in the opposite direction were sure that that kite of Bijli, which was set off at 4 a.m. would be in a cutting contest at 8 a.m. and then would sail down in the exact reverse direction. They were certain that at 8 o'clock, when crowds of children with book-bags would race towards the school, the direction of the wind would completely change, as if they were tiny oars and the wind, actually water. And the kite-catching boys that went in the direction of the wind, were certain that the wind that blew at 4 a.m. was true—like the 4 o'clock dream.

This man doesn't know if he'll be able to tell his children that hundreds of times, going against the wind for miles and, around 8 o'clock, he used to plunder Bijli's kites. And will this man's children be able to believe that the wind changes direction when children run to school? And will they believe that because he was the tallest boy, the kite would often fall into his hands?

Whenever this man gets tired of living the lives of fictional characters, he wonders if he'll be able to tell such tales to his children. Let's first assume that by telling these tales, his kite lung, engulfed in the storm of tales, will not shred. Secondly, let's also assume that the children, who were not born in the town of kites, will be able to see flying before them a fluttering image or word-picture, just by enunciating the word, 'kite'. Even after accepting both these things, will the children of this man be able to believe that in the town of kites, there are such children, on whose running together, the direction of the wind changes? And they will ask, if the direction truly changes, then do these children, also, draw gray flowers, etc.?

No, this man thinks that by relating kite-tales the issue will become so inflated that its sway will stop being visible in the sky. He should never share with his children stories which mention other children who run, race, jump, leap; who don't draw gray flowers, etc.; whose activity makes the wind turn its side. It's better, this man thinks, that he tell his wife he married her on a boast. That, in reality, he never captured any of Bijli's kites. His wife has probably not forgotten that in those days many young men used to marry on this claim.

Sometimes this man thinks that he should falsify his claim so that his wife leaves him and he doesn't have to feel the remorse of turning her out of the house.

If she leaves this man, then from this new town, he can pick another wife who doesn't have any associations with the old town. All the sorrows of the old town will splatter far away so that when the rain comes he can be happy that there's a plan for each rain drop to have its own separate path. So that he's at peace with the fact that in this town the cat doesn't go into houses to drink milk, and that the mongoose doesn't shoot out of bushes, here and there, to cross the road. So that both his eyes turn into glass and both his lungs, parrots of sand. So that the separately coursing fire and water inside him don't need shaking and blending, and the want of kneading does not feel like a lack. But then what's to be done with a wife who, despite being farsighted, agrees to wear nearsighted glasses at the slightest request? No, this, too, is not possible—the man realizes all of a sudden. So much can't change just by getting a wife from the new town. But it's also possible that he may be erecting tall arguments just to change his wife. And, maybe, the simple matter is, he's been influenced by his friend's words that after bearing two children, the wife becomes like an old, yellow chair—who, despite being the color of lime, has a body that emits the mean fragrance of green gourd.

This man kicks the table hard and topples it. At the top of his lungs, he calls to his wife to bring him the prescription that will cure him—the first sentence of which is—Just shove him off a mountain, the unformed world inside him will be stirred into shape.

The wife, at the mercy of her glasses, fumbles from toppled table to chair, chair to curtain, curtain to wall, and groping the wall, kissing the gray flowers etc. leaves the house for the first time to buy the children some colored pencils.

Sindbad

That day, too, my journey was extinguished at the well. Like everyday, I was enjoying the intoxication of sniffing at my own shadow. One nostril was assuring me that, sir, in the last thirty-two years, there has been no change in your odor. That odor, created from the slimy blend of water, moss, and frog is something of my own earning. Yet, my nostril was telling me that, very likely, the smell of my tears was no longer the same. That is because, earlier, my eye used to moisten just by witnessing a tiny little squirrel gnaw through thick vines to slip away. In those days, the slightest touch of beauty would bind me in a fine crease of light on its way back from my skin. In this same way, days of sorrow, filtering through the thin veins of leaves, used to sometimes wash my sky a clear blue. Now that doesn't happen—I had drowned the drunkenness of beauty and even the tears it brought to my eyes in the well. That's why my tears had completely changed their smell.

But, that night, I discovered some time later, that my journey hadn't been quite extinguished at the well. It didn't take me very long to find out from my other nostril that that night I wasn't alone at the well. All by myself I couldn't have figured out the age of my smiles and tears. There was someone that night whose proximity had made my tears rumble like an old man's. This was my thirty-second year at the parapet of the well. At what age did I start coming here, only the well knows. At what age will I stop coming here, this, perhaps, was known only to him who had come, and now stood leaning over my well. I don't know why I had so quickly hooked up the trivial story of my life with the sphinx-like sagacity of that man. It's just that I felt that as long as he remains standing by the well, I can go anywhere by swinging on the branches of his wander lust. The only problem was that the sounds murmuring in his ear and my ear were completely different. My ears were echoing the frog's croak at the well. His ears were resounding with oceanic storms and snowy blizzards. If the two sounds had somehow merged, we would have smiled at each other, completely disarmed. But this traveler, like a banyan, with his nightmarish roots, was swinging over my tiny, trivial root. Exactly above the croaking of the frog was his alien and unfamiliar hissing—its hood swaying from side to side.

Another problem was that after becoming the green

color of envy, I was finding it hard to change my color; although in that scheming town, I had spent my entire life getting initiation from chameleons. I began to feel myself trivialized in the same measure of the myths I had amounted about myself. Whenever, caught in the moment, I tried to pack for long romantic journeys, my luggage would suddenly seem heavier. Every minute, something would be added to it, to fix each flaw in my body. Just the thought of lifting all this weight would make the transparent fins growing on my shoulders shed and fall off. And when I postponed the journeys, my tears wouldn't dry, even after they trickled into my bones. In such a situation, to find a highly attractive traveler standing near the well was like getting caught in the earthquake that had the power to hurl me into the very core of the earth. Riding on the horn of that earthquake, I wanted to suck the ocean and forest from the jugular vein of the traveler standing beside me. Yet, I stood by, mournful and morose, even though I wanted to say with my heart and soul, that Sindbad, I've longed for you every single moment of my life. Consumed with desire, as I ran my fingers through my beard, I realized that, once again, I had been weeping into it.

Envy was showing me garden after garden of green.

At this moment, this traveler is surely looking into the eyes of a Hellenic statue and coming face to face with blind nothingness. In this nothingness, some god or the other, entering through his pores, is tangled in each of his hairs and staring at him. And now, beyond the pink windows of a cathedral, he's watching and listening to the clinking of that dewy god. And now, the breeze of a magnificent cemetery is passing above him. This breeze, showering on him the ashes of epitaphs written on the gravestones of the greatest poets, is getting buried in the setting suns. That's why, his ears are flaming red, like a fearsome poem. I want to nibble at his ear tenderly, but at this precise moment, he's riding a giant wave, like a heady sunbeam. Blinded, my eyes are watering. And now, look—he has once again landed in the city of Athens. Staggering in the darkness of a drop-dead beautiful gypsy girl, he's falling to the grass. The girl's brilliant white teeth are nibbling at my shoulders, and her hair, dissolving all the salt of my eyes, is noosing around my neck.

Despite being overwhelmed by his presence, the only name that kept dancing in my mind for this traveler was the worn out and threadbare, Sindbad. Once again I cried at my amateur romanticism. Sindbad, why can't you hear that I'm all but passionate longing for you? After tonight, will I return to this well or not—I've left that to you. If you wish, you can touch my shoulders and return the transparent fins that fell off just now. But look, your gypsy lover is still nibbling at my shoulder.

Sindbad, my master, you should just leap into me with a peculiar sound. I won't ask you to stay long. From that sound I'll know that aside from the croaking and splashing of the frog, there's the possibility that many more sounds exist—suppressed in me. And Sindbad, what's that one sound which is missing? This is the sound that'll connect me to the word whose utterance will allow me to raise my eyes to the mountains. I don't know if on the mountains there's a light for me, as well. I'm convinced, Sindbad, you know that light, because your past is all layered up with whole ranges of mountains. If you didn't know the light that's waiting eagerly for me on the mountains, then how could you have bumped into me after thirty-two years on this night, at this well? I'm certain you've seen the light that's burning, waiting for me to raise my eyes. Wait, Sindbad, I've a feeling that I'm seeing you in the dancing flame of that very light. Have you already leapt inside me? If that is so, then in the midst of all these sound waves, why is the splash of the frog the loudest. This is that frog who, from time-to-time, keeps advising me to add rigor to my romanticism, to always keep an iron bucket dipped in it, so that, whenever necessary, at least one frog in clean water can be drawn out. Yes, this is exactly what I should do, Sindbad. For a long time I've been searching for this iron bucket, in whose lack I keep imagining fins growing on my shoulders—the shedding of which makes me cry so much that even after they trickle into my bones, my tears don't dry. The splash of the frog from the well keeps sounding even in the midst of the most heavenly sounds, just like the koyal's cooing doesn't always remain in the mangroves. The constant yes of one sound and an almost constant no of the other keeps twisting my body out of shape.

I wonder when I'm capable of hearing such a subtle sound, how much more rigor does my romanticism need.

The frog's croaking directed my attention to Sindbad once again. He was standing as calmly as before, and, as soon as I saw him, I again felt that fantasy is not my strong suit. Any river that is eager to flow towards the ocean of my eyes, drowns in the sediment and dries up. This was not fantasy; this was Sindbad, for real, whom I long for every single moment of my wretched life. What was resting in cupped hands, propped on an elbow on the parapet of the well, was actually his chin that he was squeezing, as though it were some raw fruit. His blue overcoat was draining out the odor of my dirty socks. His bright magenta necktie had, for a while, been changing the colors of the nooses swinging over me. That evening, I wanted to pull one of those nooses and hang from it, but only if I could continue to see the bright magenta colors of his necktie, even after my feet were no longer on the ground. I wanted to stay like that as long as it took for the colors to become light—as long as that light, becoming sound, brought me before that word, whose utterance raised my eyes to the mountains. But my hands weren't able to lift towards his necktie. Ganga was flowing near me, and let alone wash my hands, I couldn't even gather the courage to jump into it.

In this word, 'jump,' I heard once again the inverted sound of the splash—a splash in the midst of all those sound waves, like a drowning dance of an unravelling whirlpool. Here, in my town, I had once seen a European tourist pee in some bush. As soon as he had left, I had quickly come to the site and drawn in deep breaths of that smell. But what was this? Exactly the same smell as my own stream? Even then, I had quickly peed in the wet spot and thanked god for allowing me to pee in the same patch of earth. But, somewhere inside of me, I had been singed by the fact that the wretched smell had no difference.

From the peeing incident I recalled Sindbad's necktie, connecting the two in the same way that a childhood picture is connected to an adult face. In any case, I had started to feel that Sindbad is a native man; as soon as he opens his mouth to speak, he'll break my heart. Who knows, maybe he's only been as far as the Gulf countries and now, returning lush with money and goods, has joined up with his lifeless and insipid wife. It's also possible that his overcoat is purchased second-hand on a footpath in Pakistan. I was learning to lower the iron bucket in the well. No doubt about that! But the measure of rigor that was appearing in my romanticism was the same as the shade of his magenta necktie, gesturing to me to hang myself from the tree. And, with the same intensity, I was trying to raise my eyes to the mountains. From somewhere, my mind was also sniffing at the bush, and while at it, it became petrified, because it was quite possible that he hadn't even set eyes on me yet. It was possible that that gypsy girl was actually nibbling at his shoulder with her bright white teeth, and that he was standing with his eyes closing in the voluptuous spell of her body. But this didn't mean that it wasn't Sindbad's obligation to take notice of me. Why wasn't he able to feel the intensity of the presence that he had had in my thirty-two year old history? Gypsy or no gypsy, I was there—smelly, native, and authentic—bending over on the parapet on Sindbad's left side—a beggar who had opened the sack of alms before it's time and whose golden coins had turned into frogs—who would not have thought of hanging from Sindbad's magenta necktie, if Sindbad had but touched the remainder of his life. He would have quietly returned to his wife and gone to sleep, with his head in the lap of his children, who had already become fine artists at putting him to sleep.

The thing was, I was finding it hard to change my color with the same ease with which I had slowly changed his imaginary name to reality. Believing in my I-ness, like Sindbad, had I not made myself a dubious unit? Although I knew that if Sindbad had peed before I did and had seen me smelling his pee, he would have metamorphosed into *his* mighty I-ness. The power he would have felt at this—on the basis of that—anyone, a Sindbad of any kind, would have been able to steal my place and become I. I should have the antidote for this. Just as Sindbad has a smeller on the ready on his left hand side, I should find a ready smeller on my left. Then,

I, too, can escape—just on the promise that there is someone who smells my urine—having this person, I'll better understand the stuff of my smiles and tears.

In the meantime, Sindbad, like in a bad play, burst into laughter at the wrong moment. Before I could figure out from his laughter about his traveling experiences, his language, his various pronunciations, and his urination, his hand was on my shoulder—exactly in the spot where, a little while ago, his blind-drunk gypsy lover was nibbling at my shoulder. Like a powerful magnet, he wanted to pick each mark of his lover's teeth from my shoulder. He was afraid that that girl, in her desire to acquire a language like Sanskrit, would squander her gypsy body on someone as scurrilous as I.

I have no idea what his hand was doing on my shoulder and for how long. I was faint from the pain of having gypsy teeth marks extinguished. During this time, Sindbad did mumble something to me, but I don't know in what language. Perhaps, in the language of epitaphs that can't be described in uncouth and slovenly tales. If someone tries to do it, he'll suffer the same fate as I did that night. Even after this, that wretched Sindbad didn't reveal in any way that his urine is no different from mine. Nor did he let on that he had seen me. If he had but made it evident that there is no difference in our urine, I wouldn't have agonized over the question whether he saw me or not. As soon as we meet someone, we must erase this very difference between urines, so that we can instantly trust each other. Then there won't be this great anguish about seeing-not seeing, and revealing-not revealing whether one has seen or not seen. Standing by the well that night, I realized for the first time that I'm able to philosophize with my right hand tied behind my back, although Sindbad was standing on my right hand side. So, to become a real thinker, I didn't at all need Sindbad to be present. And if I didn't, then why did I, needlessly, hook up the frivolous and vile story of my life with his sphinx-like sagacity?

But still, I had inevitably fallen for this apparition called Sindbad. To betray him would have ruined the single most significant event of my history. Sindbad, O, how insanely I long for you! With the unspoken heat of this sentence, I naively tried to fire him up one more time. But who knows, maybe at this moment he, too, is whispering this very same sentence. Perhaps he has taken me to be Sindbad and is now secretly longing for me. It's possible that he has turned up in my town, straight from a mesmerizing site in Europe, intending to acquire a smattering of Sanskrit and has now planted himself directly at my well. Who knows, maybe at this precise moment, he, too, is thinking of me as the Sindbad of Sanskrit, and he, too, finds it difficult to change his green color of envy. In my mind, I started reciting the Gita to him, and in my heart, enraptured, I heard the beautiful blue blink of his eyes. The more he got entangled in the shlokas, the higher up I sat in the chariot. Sitting there, I completely forgot that I didn't know the first thing about Sanskrit. But what difference does that make—what difference did it make to me whether he was a traveler or not? My mind is murmuring; and isn't that enough?

But, in the meantime, the magenta necktie was ready in his other hand, in the shape of a half noose, exactly in the same way that my own brown necktie would have been ready in a half noose a little while ago, if I had remained in my chariot. But now the game was entirely in Sindbad's hand. My time had come.

As soon as the game suddenly goes into the other person's hand, your attention is broken by the myths you have churned about yourself and the innocuous little story that floats up.

After the story broke, I discovered that I had forgotten the croaking of the frog in the story itself. It's not that it was the sound of a splash, which I would need to retrieve with the iron bucket. The smell of pee, too, had flowed out of my heart and completely emptied. With absolute intensity, I was now living out that ritual, which, joining my brown necktie to the bright magenta tie, was taking the shape of a noose in Sindbad's hand. I was ready to offer myself.

But then I saw Sindbad himself go toward the tree with the noose in his hand. Perhaps, that wasn't a tree at all; it was the lap of Sindbad's children, hanging from which his feet would soon be dangling above the earth.

In the void, through my pores, God was rising in every single hair of my body.

Just a Story

A fish bone is stuck inside me. There's no pain—just a thorny feeling that neither grows nor lessens. My feet, like easy oars, are busy rowing me along. Each part of my body seems to be flowing. In the wind, water and earth, beyond any pain, my body is drifting without any effort. Only, every once in a while, the fish bone shudders—like a piece in a machine that someone has left running and then closed the factory.

Up till now I have only come to know that I've left the hospital. Some tubes must still be hanging from my nostril—I have a feeling. My wounds are still oozing—what is oozing from them is trickling down my body like cold sweat. I should look behind me right away to see if there's any animal licking the drops that have dripped. I should find out what condition I'm in, because I'm unable to figure it out from the pain. Whatever I am now—body or something else—pain has no interest in it.

I'm lucky that I still have the illusion that my memory is fine. For example, at least I remember that that night they hadn't admitted my wife to the labor room. They had told her to remain in the veranda. The nurse had punched her belly and examined her."It's only the fifth month," she had shouted. "Will you now sprawl here for four months, or come back to the hospital when it's time to open the damned bundle?" A nine-month belly was sprawled before me but sleep was pressing on me so much that I thought it best to just believe the nurse. Although, if I had shot just a pebble, my wife's full crock-pot would have burst and that butter-thief blue god himself would have manifested on the veranda of the hospital. But, at the moment—sleep.

I have no idea how, that night, my wife managed to get to the toilet. The light bulb was missing, and there, struggling in the darkness, she began to burst with pain. By the time the cleaning woman arrived with the lantern, the infant was hanging in the flush. The empty body birthing it had keeled forward. Cursing, the cleaning woman yelled loudly why the witch had stunk up the toilet, and then she began tearing away the clothes from the body that had keeled over, beating it with both hands from time to time. Everything was tangled up between them—the cleaning woman and my wife. My wife and the infant dangling below from her umbilical cord. The infant and the gushing flush. The lantern smoke braiding the streaming blood into ropes. The ropes reeking humid of petroleum, and I, tied up in that humid reek, standing with hands folded in the doorway of the toilet.

No, I felt no desire to save my wife in this film. And, in the midst of the beating-battling and pulling and yanking, the child had fallen silent.

But the effect was this, that on seeing the cleaning woman, I became enamored with her. I was holding myself responsible for her insanity, and like an insane person myself, I was also an outsider to her insanity. But with all my heart, I wanted to be a part of it. However, before I could do anything, the same nurse, who had punched my wife's stomach and had declared that it was only the fifth month, arrived there. She glared at me as though I myself had started this horror film, and then to embarrass the nurse had made my wife act the role of a woman who has just given birth. She was perhaps also thinking that I had even forced her to play her own role of nurse so that she could see her humiliation displayed on the whole screen. We were both in the process of glaring at each other, when suddenly, she completely read on my face the terrifying attraction to the cleaning woman. Then, making noise with her starched white uniform, she cut through the dark corridor, spilling the glitter of a fallen star behind her. Closing my eyes in that glitter, I wished for one thing—that by the time I came to end, I would still remember my wish.

As soon as the film ended, I went to the veranda and joined the other snores. Just like I remember all the snores that were sprawled on the veranda of the hospital that night, I remember, by heart, all the moles and scars of childhood wounds on my wife's body. I even remember her mother's, whose body I had bathed and prepared for the funeral. The reason I had bathed my mother-in-law's body was because my wife had been unconscious, and some people, holding bowls of curd, had wanted to participate in the ritual in a way that would have enabled them to examine the moles and childhood scars of the corpse's daughter.

When they brought my wife and the crushed infant to me for identification, they brought them wrapped in the stink of the toilet. Employed in an ammonia factory, stink was something I had worked very hard to earn. I had no trouble identifying. If they had wanted, I could have related verbatim, all the marks, including childhood scars, on my wife's body. If they had wanted, I would have opened the baby's closed fist and tried to tell them its future. Just like I used tell all those who used to work with me in the ammonia factory. In the dirt coated lines of their palms I used to read them stories of their air and oceanic journeys, lotteries that were dying to be declared winners, the prosperity of their children, and their loyalty. They too would flock around me everyday, as though in a matter of twenty-four hours their fate had brightened a great deal and they thought it their duty to show it to me. They and I were repeatedly caught watching the same Bombay-esque film in the theater of the same destiny.

In any case, when the two were brought to me for identification, I felt the same craving to open the baby's fist that I had felt to wash my mother-in-law's body in curd. Outside the hospital, pigeons were declaring 8 a.m. in the clock tower. This was the only way left for me to know time. The spot for the number 8 was covered with pigeon droppings. The newspaper deliverers had delivered the newspapers and returned. People, everywhere, were reading news items, whose commas and periods were not reminding them of the moles and scars that I knew by heart. At the time of identification, I had nodded my head slightly to acknowledge that this was my wife and our child, who had been found in a pulp on her body. I had even recognized those flies that were sitting on the lips of the infant.

But now the cleaning woman. The third-eye opening broom. The paling tree of my craze now only demanded her water. She had beaten and torn apart my wife's clothing and body parts, but the umbilical cord had remained unbroken. I, too, wasn't broken. With my hands tied, I could enter the world's most terrifying mountain pass, haunted mansion, well of death; all at the merest gesture from the cleaning woman. After all, who, even after paying a high price, can tell whether he's on the side of the cleaning woman or of the baby pulp hanging in the flush? And then, I hadn't even paid that high a price. Let alone ammonia, no chemical of the world, nor poison can hurt me now. But I can't forget those tragedies that used to cause the death of my friends and their children. When spring was in its youth, so many times the fragrance of mango blossoms and the oozing smell of ammonia used to run into each other. And then under white sheets, the swollen bellies of children. These children were the same whose shining futures I used to read in the hands of the workers. Exactly as someone reads the letters of his beloved in the light of Bombay-esque films. The deaths that happened in the gas tragedy would touch me like time touches wounds. That's why I felt the craving to open the fist of the flush-toilet baby. But I only made an acknowledgement.

My head nodded and I realized that aside from ammonia, there is no other truth on the earth. To approach that truth I'll have to peek inside the belly of the cleaning woman. Or inside someone's half-swept heart that cries out to kill women, like my wife, who had just given birth. Where the smell of ammonia gobbles up the fragrance of mango and burps. But at least I felt consoled that being on the cleaning woman's side, I wouldn't even have to bother lifting a broom to sweep, so as to get to the truth.

But why won't I need to bother? Even after the cleaning woman swept my mind, it's filled with trash. It's true that she tore apart my wife and child—but why? Can I understand the reason via some other form of relationship. For example, the relationship between a mother and infant? Take that mother, who, to cure her child's bad stomach, spits chewed fennel seeds in its mouth. The mother's inclination for baby flesh! Drawing away from the baby's lips, how many times must she wish to chew them up—stuff the crunching pink sound in her mouth, like fresh carrots. And, it's possible that while she does this, her thighs become sweaty. Her breasts become tightened for suckling. At this time, she feels no need for a man; with just a little help from the baby, she is within herself both male and female. This whole process—that man who is only man and not woman at all, or that woman who is only woman; not man at all—any indifferent being who claims to be a total male or female—calls this whole play between a mother and child maternal love. Nature has not given human beings a bigger delusion than this. The delusions that serve nature's purpose are the delusions that we receive. And when we don't receive them, we fall prey to delusions. But when it's declared in the war that Ashvathaman has been killed, I understand that it's the elephant that's been killed. In the stories woven by human beings, this is the precise relationship between humans and elephants.

But despite being guilty of killing the elephant, I'm on the outside. Completely untouched and untouchable. Like the cleaning woman. I am trying to lull and subdue—the many untouchable, untouched tangled snakes in my belly. Those innocent beings, who are only either male or female, can call this sympathy. I, too, can call it this; except that I'll have to change the beginning of my story—in which there is no tragedy at the hospital—there is no mention of the wife's tiny attractive moles. I should accept, without hesitation, that I remember by heart all those moles that are still glowing on that wretched woman's body, like my insanity. But, if my wife and child hadn't been pulled into the labyrinths of the nurse and the cleaning woman in the hospital, would I have been able to talk about the minutest details of the melody of the natural world, about the dew-lined and poison-domed or, else, some fine silver-enameled spectacular ruins, as before? Would I have been able to differentiate between the quiet created by the falling of the tree and one's silence while facing the sea? These are the lines along which my aesthetic might have run if I had but changed the beginning of my story.

But if I believe that I have changed the beginning of the story, and there is no hospital in my new story, nor is there the death of my wife and baby, even then would I have not met the cleaning lady on some other pretext, in some other house or hut? Would I have not discovered that I'm an ordinary worker in the ammonia factory, who has seen innumerable children lying row after row under white sheets in the tragedies of the gas leak? Seeing these, hasn't my mouth been salivating? That saliva, drool, or hunger that can be fed back into the machine and made into ammonia after ammonia? What is the relationship between drool and the production of ammonia? Can I reach the cleaning woman's venomous snakes with the help of this relationship? No. Once again I have fallen prey to delusion. I shouldn't forget that I'm outside. I'm untouched. Undecaying. Immortal. Standing outside the giant building of natural harmony, I'm a massive plot against gravity. If I'm not, then how am I standing outside the building?

But then it is also possible that there was never any plot against me. There was no hospital in my history. My wife and the infant crushed in the toilet were never real. I just started a story. It's as though, dreaming about catching fish in my pee, I got wrapped in the arm of an octopus. In the midst of eight arms, a red mouth is rapidly pulling me towards itself. For as long as I'm being pulled, I'll keep blabbering.

Really, nothing was real. The moles on my wife's body and the scars from her childhood wounds, that were evident on her knees like fossils of juicy fruits—all of them were really the dreams of the snakes in my belly. Playing with words, I wasn't able to reach there, where, in colloquial language, you need to be sympathetic.

In other words, to feel sympathy, I should have actually

been a worker in the ammonia factory. I lied that I am. But I also know that if I don't get to the factory by tomorrow or the day after, I'll lose my job. I don't even know in which direction is the factory in this town. Is it in the middle of a heavily populated area, or is it there where, around the factory, unemployed shacks spring up overnight like wild mushrooms? After the tragedies in the factory, different newspapers print different accounts. Under the list of announced casualties, it's stated that the above list doesn't include the list of unknown people. I can see clearly how we were made 'unknown.' My ears can still hear the splash—the splash of all those dead and unconscious who were thrown in the water from the bridge. Oh, there is so much peace in this sound. Ammonia, did I say? I don't remember the name of that lung-tearing smell. But I do remember the name of the raag that was being played on the sitar at that time. Ah, how sweet was the gust of maalkauns that was dissolving in each wave as people were being flung into the water.

I don't know the music-sense of cattle. Their bellies had swollen with gas, and it was not as easy to lift them and throw them as it was with us. They had become bigger than life.

But in the root of these scenes, is ammonia the only

gas present? Or is it just being called ammonia? I have no idea what is the actual effect of ammonia, or any other gas, on plants, people, and buffaloes. Ammonia is not a thing from the inside of nature's melody. Like me, it's outside this melody. Yet, the word 'root' is bothering me. But why ever am I still stuck on words?

Roots! And now trunk...that which is stretched between trunk and leaves—even that I haven't yet been able to find. The grand mansion of natural harmony that was before me just now, outside of which I had, for a moment, fully experienced my presence, where is it? It seems that someone is trying to forcibly pull me outside, across the doorjamb. I'm stuck—am I a bovine animal swollen with gas? What actually is this pulling? Am I being pulled towards the mouth of the octopus? And am I blabbering away as I get pulled?

After identifying my family at the hospital, I don't know why I was arrested by the police. I was already beginning to talk rubbish. And then I was getting beaten, and on the curtain of my swollen eyes, I saw the beautiful unique faces of those people who were clinging to that trunk, which I still haven't been able to find. Ammonia (that is a pseudo name for roots) and the trunk among the burgeoning leaves, that wasn't a trunk at all. Instead of the trunk, I saw the innocent, sad facial features of many privileged and divine beings. Lightly burnt in God's dazzle, their lips were moving slightly in prayer. While getting beaten up, I even tried to sharpen my ears so as to hear their prayers. Words I couldn't hear. To hear God's word was probably not an ailment of my ears—this is what I thought. But from this practice, at least I found out that they too suffer intensely even though they're clinging to the trunk. Why should I live in this arrogance that I'm the only one who suffers tangled in the roots—I, who at this time, am a swollen bovine—who doesn't achieve Oneness through singing and dancing and prayer.

Truly, if I could have learned the essential meaning of their prayers, then the whole tree would have become truth. But it's certain that they too must suffer and agonize—those who are blissfully unaware that in this world, the name of one root of sorrow can also be ammonia. Those who don't know that a leaf borne by the root can also be the cleaning woman. Ammonia and cleaning woman, etc—words that have forcibly become my share—words with which I have started a beginning that I never should have. In the middle, like transient saints clinging to the invisible trunk, I've been changing my images like slough. But I didn't change the snake. It is the same snake that's in the belly of the cleaning woman—in the belly of the same cleaning woman who, becoming a terrible sun, is dancing on the precipice of my desire. She, too, will soon sink. Whose sorrow like a fishbone winces in my soul, without any pain. This is the very place where I had started my story. If it had been another place, then perhaps, I wouldn't have had to live through this day.

If, at this moment, someone spontaneously asks to me to show a glimpse of my wife's moles and scarred knees, I'll say, not now. If someone spontaneously asks me why I didn't open the fist and read the fate lines of the infant hanging crushed from the umbilical cord, then I'll say, ask those praying people who are clinging to the tree trunk. I'm impatient to hear their views on this subject, just as, right now, the center of the octopus is impatient for me. If someone says to me that he can give me a glimpse of the whole tree—just one glimpse of the truth of the whole tree, then I'll even be prepared to crush the scorched leaf whose name is cleaning woman—despite the fact that her desire is licking at me like a hellish thirst. Forgetting her, I want to see that tree trunk whose moisture and darkness she has drunk from inside the damp wood, and changed into a scorched leaf.

When she was changing, subtle-minded people, clinging to the tree trunk, must have experienced her for a moment and left her. They must have seen her in some corridor of a hospital carrying a can of phenol, and they must have gotten tangled up in the hooded cobras depicted on the can. They must have seen her outside a shack, picking lice from the hair of an old hag, and they must have extracted their sad sun from her glowing copper. They must have heard her buzzing in some bus stand toilet, and instead of giving her a ten paisa coin had handed her a one rupee coin. Then the rest of their journey must have passed, warmed in the womb of their generosity. She must have passed by them and from inside them so many times—for a long time—but dividing her on the scale of seconds, they must have fogged up the process of her scorching, the same way that I wouldn't have felt the growing of the tree if I had but gotten a glimpse of its totality.

Perhaps, this is only right; those who are immersed in transient prayers near the tree—from them, those who are grappling with the root named ammonia, should be kept away. It is desirable for scorched leaves to remain untouched. But then, this, too, is my delusion that every incident, accident, birth, death, sin, virtue and its effect in this world can be understood through the medium of the tree. If this were so, then, during my beating, when they were trying to make me divulge the names and addresses of my cohorts, wouldn't I have blurted out the names of those who, with such innocence and sincerity, were clinging to the sides of the trunk immersed in prayer? Why did only those names spill out of my mouth who were battling the roots of ammonia with me, who they wanted to apprehend on the charge of some workers' strike. Or perhaps, these were the same names that had been buried in the unknown persons' list in the aftermath of the gas leak.

These are the very names, whose compensation applications will be filled by some stranger's hand and a big hand will clean up. Those very names who after giving birth to handicapped children have left them at the mercy of green flies. All this can't be understood from the symbol of the tree. If this were possible, then during my beating I would have definitely blurted out the scorching whose destiny is ultimately to merge once again with the root of ammonia.

If that scorched leaf was dancing like a terrible sun on the precipice of my desire; now it is sinking. By now my name must have faded in the factory's register. After the police beating, how long did I sleep with hospitals tubes, needles and cylinders? Who should I ask here? I can see that all the pigeons sitting above the clock in the clock tower, are now heaped right below the hands showing 6 o'clock. From here, I can't tell exactly whether they are dead, sleeping, or on their collective eggs displaying collective maternal love. If there are eggs under them, then the poisonous gas in the air must certainly have wandered through them—the smell which is the sum total of what I have earned. In a little while, close to the clock-hands of seven or eight o'clock, hopping baby pigeons will fall down dead all by themselves. Seeing the place of their death, I will, even after one or two hours, be able to read today's time in the clock tower.

If it is six in the evening, then my night shift is about to begin. But is this the same town in which my ammonia factory is located? It's hard to tell. If I'm a worker, then my name can be found in the register, even if it's faded. Is this any less of a belief? If I'm a dead bovine animal whose belly has swollen with gas, and people are trying to pull me across some door jamb, then I should just shut up. Maybe by keeping quiet, I'll shrink and silently help the workers who are trying to pull at me. Who knows, perhaps the factory and the beautiful mansion of natural harmony that I don't know in what segment of time I saw—are actually just different postures of the same place. But in the meantime, in which direction am I smelling gas? Have I really been swallowed by the octopus' mouth? Then, with the end of the process of pulling, my babbling must also be coming to an end. In all eventualities, this is the indication for me, that now it's time to end. If my beginning was true, then I must reach somewhere, while I still smell the gas. It appears that one more tragedy has struck in another town.

I know I am arriving there. From here, afar, I can see rows of swollen bellies piled up for miles under white sheets. My drool, in the shape of the same river, has already reached under the sheets of children.

With this drool, I want to pay homage to what I call natural harmony. If I call this sympathy, then I'll only have to change the beginning. And that, too, only of one story. Just by changing the beginning of one story, someone's wife and child won't die.

Suparna and I

Outside in the tamarind tree Sanwla is sitting. You can see the tree from this room. It's a room made of glass. I am here, in this glass room, with Suparna. Anyone sitting in the tree can now see there are two women in this room. Suparna and I.

Suparna reminds me that I'm very tired. It's this tiredness that brings me back to this room. All I have to keep in mind is that I'm tired. Suparna is quiet and is looking at me. My heart begins to beat loudly. Suparna at once turns her glance away; there's nothing she doesn't know. We'll begin whenever you wish to, she breaks her silence. I don't know what it is that Suparna wishes. You could, if you like, slowly take off your clothes, I'll give you a massage. The moment Suparna utters these words, I begin to feel extremely tired all over again. All I have to remember, somehow, is that I am tired. Looking at me, she utters yet another word. This word reminds me of nothing. Only the sound of it casts a spell of warmth over my limbs. Can I ask her what it is that should come to my mind on hearing this word?

—Why don't you lie down, I'll be back in a minute.

I go and lie down—in the tenderness of Suparna's utterance, leaning on my own tiredness. Suparna is removing a mirror from the glass wall. I know I've never seen anything like this before—a human form removing a mirror from a glass wall. Across the mirror only those images will flash that you're able to remember. If you don't remember anything, all you'll see are these glass walls and a misty milklight hanging from the ceiling. Having taken the mirror from the wall, Suparna has placed it next to me on the floor.

Suparna's glance takes in that I'm lying on the floor, just like that. She's not in a hurry. She doesn't have to go anywhere. What comfort is this sentence!—*She does not have to go anywhere.* I don't know why it's so comforting to think that the one who is with me at the moment doesn't have to go anywhere. The mirror lying next to me has no images from my memory. I remember nothing that will flash across this mirror. Only the glass walls around me. And the bulb-shaped milky cloud-like light hanging from the ceiling. *There is light here,* I tell myself.

Craning my neck I see that there is a tamarind tree outside. In the dense cluster of branches, Sanwla sits, surrounded by the dangling pods. The pods are his matted locks. Now I can see Suparna sliding out of her costume. Have I ever seen anything like this before? But I know why she's doing this. She knows that my body is not unaffected. Clothes exist, I'm grateful. The illusion of hiding remains intact, I'm grateful. But, sure enough, Suparna is now shedding her skin with the beauty of a glass snake. In the light from a milky cloud, a glass snake is rising from within its own body. And now her limbs fill up with human colors. If Suparna had been of dusky complexion, I would have been able to see her well enough in this glass room. And yet I'm able to see the twenty-two year old Suparna sliding out of her clothes like a child so that I, too can, shed my shackles. Should I look at you, Suparna, keep looking at you, or gaze into the mirror instead?

Without looking at the tamarind tree, and looking only at Suparna, I can feel Sanwla's eyes burning on Suparna. In a little while, surely, he will look at me, too. But not the way he looks at Suparna. He'll perceive the lack of sap in my limbs. What has vanished he will witness in the presence of that which is there. At sap that is filled with tenderness. In the glass room, he's going to witness a subtle event about to unfold in a human body. Sanwla won't keep looking at me. Won't be able to. Images that were once so enchanting fall to the ground the moment they are bereft of form.

Sanwala won't be able to stop looking at Suparna. At sap, at light, at tenderness. Sitting in the darkness and flavor of the tree, he'll long for Suparna. She's sitting on her haunches. Inebriated by what her body bids me, I loosen the hundreds of strings fastened around me. My hair has been done into countless tiny braids. My tired fingers begin to undo these braids. Loosening so minutely, I get deeply absorbed. Like an angel of undoing, I, too, slowly slide out of my intricate costume. My shoulders no longer droop to cover me. I'm at peace. Tired, but at peace. Face down, I stretch myself before Suparna. Her hair caresses me as if I were asleep under the fragrance of a wave. With nimble fingers she begins to massage me from head to toe, making tiny, gentle whirlpools all over me. In order to feel her touch at all I have to stay wide awake in the sleep within sleep. But there's no effort involved in this. No initiation either. To stay awake in the inner circle of sleep is as easy as staying asleep in the outer circle without Suparna's touch.

Suparna, I ask, *it isn't as if our room is in the middle of a public square?*

It is, says Suparna.

I hear my mother's voice explaining to the woman next-door that her daughter is very tired and rather unwell. That she is lying like this so that she can get a proper massage. I hear the voice of the woman next-door: okay, I see how it is. But that woman who is giving her the massage, why is she without clothes? I strain my ears to listen to my mother. But I don't hear her voice. Then, all at once, surrounded by several voices, I hear my mother's sobs: *I don't know, I know nothing.*

Her sobs, Suparna, do you think I'll have the strength?

Suparna says, now you should lie down on your back. She begins to make tiny whirlpools around my navel. Surrounded by the same voices in the mirror is now Suparna's voice. She is asking my mother's neighbor to keep quiet. My mother's sobs once again rise to a high pitch, and then fall silent.

Suparna has now handed over the mirror to me. On my neck, the same whirling downpour of Suparna's voice, her breathing, and her touch. In the mirror my mother's sobs are now beginning to encircle me. Next time, before she begins, I have to present myself to her in a way that she doesn't start all over again.

On my eyelids, Suparna's caress. Her lips. My whole body is flooded with tears. My eyes don't allow them. Ripping through the poetry of this dream, all I want to do is kiss Suparna's eyes.

This room is right in the middle of a public square. In the mirror I see the woman who is my mother's neighbor.

Suparna's lips are being drenched with my tears. She lets them.

In the mirror, another woman now. Covered in a dirty veil of muslin, she suddenly stops at the threshold of my childhood home. In the second reading I've removed the sentences that were once here.

In the mirror they have placed my father's body before the woman in a dirty muslin veil. I said, *placed.* Had someone wanted, they could also say they made my father lie down in her presence. But my father can no longer use the enchanting words he had coined. A big cart loaded with ice screeches to a halt at the entrance. The cart man says, *Where do I offload this ice, is this the house?*

Is this the house? I whisper into the mirror. The woman in the muslin veil tells the other women who have now thronged the courtyard that he was young as *kadi*. What on earth are these words they're using for my father? I have no idea what *kadi* means. She says, not a single gray hair, think of that. A shadow passes quickly over my childhood home. Drenching me, another phrase sails past me. *Sâyâyé-abré-guréźâ.**

I'm in the middle of circling waves. There is Suparna. And very deep waters. Over me a boat freeing itself of the whirlpool has drifted away. I try to swim my way in the whirlpool. I don't want to surface, because I have to hide myself from view. Water trickles into my lungs and my mind dips into calmness. I don't wish to surface and begin to hear my mother's voice. Now my brother's too. They are turning my name into screams.

This is the first ever time my name has been turned into screams. This is the first ever time I hear my own name in this play, and it doesn't sound strange to me. My name is like someone close to me who wishes to get drowned along with me. Somehow it has to be extricated from my mother's and brother's loud pitch. But it's they who have made the first move. I've been dragged out

* Shadows of drifting clouds.

of the river. There's one *I* who is being pulled by the fisherwomen into a boat. There's another *I*, who, standing on the riverbank without any clothes on, is explaining to my mother why it's important to remain in this state.

My mother and my brother look now at me, now at my body in the boat. They burst into loud wailing. My mother is trying to explain something to the people gathered on the riverbank. No one betrays any sign of having grasped anything. She tries yet another time. She says the one in the boat is not her daughter, the one who has drowned, and whom the fisherwomen have placed in the boat. Her daughter, she says, is standing right here, on the riverbank. Tired and sick, she has removed her clothes, says mother...then mother's words are missing. The ones that are missing I know by heart; they have always been the same—*How many times do I have to tell her not to wear her father's clothes. Is this the way to be in mourning that you keep chasing men who are like your father?* Suparna is nowhere in sight. I stand on the riverbank flanked by my mother and brother and try to feel Suparna's touch like a breeze on my skin. Suparna, I say softly, and despite wanting to, I can't make my eyes well up with tears.

Whatever has happened is because of the woman next-door—my mother's voice. *It's her questions in which my child has drowned.* The woman next-door is saying, *but that's what your daughter was like.*

My mother and my brother are together in an underground room. What I have on is heavy winter clothing. I tell them I'm not on my way somewhere. It strikes me how easily they trust my word. In the same breath I plead with someone that they should put it off no longer, that they should push me off the edge of the roof now. From somewhere the smell of my father's last medicines wafts up to me. Over the parapet, on the terrace, a bouquet of rays comes into play. This is the precise spot where I have to begin my descent. My mother shouldn't weep. My limbs grow heavy with her wailing. Why doesn't she know this is not the way. She has no idea how to read the signs of light. She can't read, this mother of mine. She knows nothing.

At a street-corner stands a home for lepers. I tell my brother that it's here he could leave some money. He's walking by my side with a tenth of his salary stashed in his pocket. Even in this state I walk with a matter-of-fact face, as if I'm well acquainted with the home for lepers. For a moment it crosses my mind that transactions here are not quite above-board. But having pointed the place out to my brother, I can't express doubt now. My brother listens very attentively to me and stops for a moment to figure out the location. Even then he says, *when you're no longer here, will I still be able to recognize this place?*

The stairs to the third floor of my granny's house. Every step is scarred by cracks that I don't like. A peepal tree has already taken root in a crevice. In the mirror I hear my mother's voice—*when you were about to be born I had seen a cobra on this very step. If a woman with child happens to sight a snake, it goes blind. It had slithered away into this very hole. This peepal wasn't there then. The moment it vanished into the hole, your grandpa poured boiling hot oil into the chink.* Boiling hot oil, grandpa? It's me over whom you've poured the oil; could it have been you, grandfather?

On every step, the sound of its writhing hood. Right over this sound, on each step, and covering the crevices, there stands a chef. A whole line of chefs, one on each step, arrayed on the entire staircase. They stand stiffly in their dazzling white uniforms. A cauldron of boiling oil in front of each one of them. An aroma of sea-foods invades the steps. The fragrance of green fenugreek is absent, but still lingers somewhere. That's all I can make out. Even so, I want to hold on to the entire range of aromas lingering here. The pointed red crests of the caps worn by the chefs pierce the rainbows arching overhead.

In the three-storey house of my grandma, on every step of the uppermost staircase, there is only one scene repeated on seventeen steps—a chef standing in white uniform—the crest touching the arch of the rainbow overhead. Seventeen boiling cauldrons. Seventeen rainbows that could fall any moment into the oil. Deep inside every step, the sound of a writhing snake-hood. Placing a hand on my belly I try to diminish my hurt. This turns out to be Suparna's hand.

The mirror shows my mother and my brother walking. I keep wiping the fog off the mirror. My memory surfaces, rippling in the reflection—a deluge of images.

Superna rises from the floor, gathering her hair.

Taking the mirror from my hand, she hangs it back on the glass wall.

Su

Even in those twenty-one pages that are written and lying on the table, Su isn't there. In the rear room, Su's white shirt is lying in the iron box. Su's fragrance is not in the shirt either. It was raining in those days.

Su is not on the verandah where the blue chairs are.

When the siesta is broken, if you gaze in the empty air for a while, Su is there sometimes.

Rumi is beyond comforting. My sniffing at Su's shirt. My gaze in the empty air when the siesta is broken.

But if one gets up and writes him down right away, it's possible that he does get written. By feeling this, Su sometimes remains; in the possibility of meeting Su, while attempting to write down aching limbs, there is Su.

Rumi's eyes are brimming with venom and sorrow.

I had no clue I would try to visualize Su tearing through the air, as soon as Su left the verandah sculpted from those five days. Had no clue I would try to excavate and sniff him out from the fragrance of the white shirt he had forgotten in the rear room. That I would keep wiping the water from my eyes and nose with his white shirt. That the moment he left, Tanya would wave at me with the white shirt Su had forgotten in the rear room, and that I would snatch it out of her hands the very same minute, with force. Had no clue that, sorrowing, a body could harbor so much violence.

I couldn't have guessed that the morning after those five nights Su would ask me if, in a few days time, I would go to see him off at the big city airport, and I would say no.

I had no clue that when Su called me the following night from the big city, I would name the city of Bharatpur to meet him halfway, even in that heavy downpour. Nor did I know that the same night in his kitchen, Rumi would keep staring at a knife he had bought to slice bread.

That same night, talking to him on the phone, Kumar would hear the sound of the sea in Rumi's sobs.

At three in the morning, my train halts at the rainy platform at Bharatpur station. I had gotten off the train in the pitch darkness of the last station and, walking in the rain, had asked a lantern, Brother, is this Bharatpur? No one would tell me whether it was Bharatpur or not, not even the three passengers in my coach who had to get off at Bharartpur. I had no idea that the platform at Bharatpur would be flooded with light and that it would be possible to read the name Bharatpur even through sheets of rain.

I had no clue that the possibilities of Su's being there and his not being there would shred my body in the same way.

I had no clue his glasses would have the same mist; that even drenched, he would appear as though his skin had the same warmth. He would smile. Trying not to fall asleep, he would get off at Bharatpur. In his blue bag would be a book by Marina Tsvetayeva...I had no clue.

At four in the morning, and then at six, an attempt to enter the bird forest in the light drizzle.

Trees and bushes shooting up from the water-bodies of birds, drops shedding from leaves on the backs of birds that looked like boats. Bidis begged from rickshaw pullers. A thatched kiosk selling chai near the Shiva temple. Under the tower, a cot of jute string. Eight cups of tea. From the samovar of Dostoevsky.

Only if we close the several books between Su and I, will he able to leave.

Su should not have accompanied me to Rumi's place. But considering the disarming transparency of his face, he could very well do so. *When Rumi reads it in my face, he won't be sad,* Su says. In Su's face, there are no lines that cause sadness. Rumi reads a bit too much these days between lines and in faces. With his reading, my face flushes with warmth. Su's face won't be able to bear Rumi's reading. The lines will break. Even then Su will keep fiddling with my glasses lying on Rumi's mat. Facing Rumi's venom and sorrow, he will continue to wipe my glasses with his handkerchief.

That every sentence will be a slight lie in which I'll place Su? Will keep circling that dome in a way that Su is visible and yet not visible? Will play with beads of lies and Su's departure will be like blood rising in the air, above the danger mark?

The word Su will be such that the silencing of all other sounds will be Su. In a way that Su will be sleeping behind that word that is stretched out in Su's shape on the page. The moment you utter Su, the Su breeze will begin to blow. The moment you utter Su, Su would dissolve in his own reflection. The word Su will be as if a white page were just beginning to talk to itself in solitude.

He speaks in white, smiles in white.

I asked him what he would do sitting in my tiny little place for five days. I have Marina Tsvetayeva, Su said.

Su sits reading Marina quietly the whole day.

Su is invisible. It takes hard work to remember to make his food. He manages to sleep on a diwan much too small for him. With him around, my face can form lines that are no different from the ones when I'm alone. He has no history of love. I don't have to be onstage. I'm not at all prepared for this play.

During these five days his departure is in the making at my place and, before he departs, so is his ability to be seen in his absence. By the time I find this out it'll be too late. I don't know what it means when I say this. This is the first event of its kind, and no prior sentences have been formed for it—no syntax.

Su is visible in a way that I'm able to see the space devoid of him once he leaves. That space is slowly lighting up, which I'm soon going to inhabit. I'll never leave this space. I won't even need to take a shower anymore. It won't be right to even unravel my tangled hair. And ants will soon come crawling to my numb arms.

It's perhaps not possible to write this down. That the body will long to be in a space where a few sentences can be formed. Su, himself… these days is the lack of those same sentences.

Rumi's venom and sorrow glare at me. To get me to utter those sentences.

And then there's one Marguerite who can write a story without any incident. The incidents she writes about can't be seen. A blue breeze.

She doesn't go anywhere. With the door bolted shut she keeps lying with her face towards the sea. She is made of the sounds of the sea, of the lights playing on the sea. She's begun to linger on the edges of death. Even so, all the lovers are still sixteen or seventeen years old. She's even beginning to write without memory. This Marguerite.

She's the only one who knows how to write without memory. On her pages is all that she keeps seeing streaming in the siesta air. It's between her lines that sometimes I get to see Su.

Whenever he's seen, he's beyond bearing. Even in Marguerite's lines. Fyodor's Myshkin surfaces in the blank spaces between Marguerite's lines. He's not in the white pages lying on my table.

To see him one has to open a page of Marguerite. I see in which particular detail Su sometimes forms in Marguerite's pages. In which blank space his eyes, his breathing. Once again, in Marguerite's pages, he is written by me—Su.

On the stairs to my verandah is a thin layer of last night's rain. That sound-picture was too dark and windy in which Su and I had sat framed in the verandah. We had blue chairs and the entire night to ourselves. The rain was on our faces, where it was dark. In the windstorm, water and lightning flashed every now and then. The eucalyptus trees shone. Laden with yellow blossoms, the trees shone. Up in the trees there was the sleep of peacocks on storm-tossed branches. In the framed verandah, the windstorm struck like a picture. Between the lightning flashes, Su could be seen sometimes, sometimes not.

This was the third night. I'm trying to write Su for the third time.

Su is sitting with his face lifted to the eucalyptus trees. He will see the peacocks descending into the garden, in the cold picture of dawn breaking. In the layer of rain on the steps, I see the reflection of peacocks. In a little while I'll see their short, clumsy flights in the mirror of rainwater. Su will see them descending from the sky between the branches. Then he'll go to sleep. He'll rise from his blue chair… so will I. He'll smile.

There's another night left. He should have died before this last night.

While I sit writing this last sentence, at this very moment—Su's phone. Impossible! But, it's not surprising. It's likely that the sentences I've deleted, Su is speaking from there. Not he, but his nightlong drunken voice. Leaving the party and thinking of calling me from the next room—that Su. As if he were still thinking —that kind of voice. As if he were not being able to hear me. *That girl who reads Marguerite,* says Su, *that Marguerite woman I spoke to you about, she's also here attending the party. She wanted to sit with me in a circle of earthen lamps this evening.*

In Su's geography, it's again midnight. Here, the first winter rain and afternoon. I get envious. In your voice, it's always night.

Marguerite can write you just by hearing your voice on the phone. Even after her own death in March she says she can write you from your phone voice.

Her Chinese lover is on the phone. After sixty four years. His voice from his own house in China in the midst of other voices. The voice that jolted Marguerite's fifteen year old body out of sleep.

Then even that voice is not there. She has just heard that he's no more…His passing has turned Marguerite into a novelist, yet again. Marguerite is happy. She won't write leaning on the memory of days when she was also in love with her younger brother. It was easy to tell lies to Mother.

What could those sentences have been? That lie?

Rumi walks in the middle of the road in heavy traffic. He's not able to crush Su in his heart. Drivers stop their buses and shove him to the pavement by cussing him out.

Holding on to Kumar's voice on the phone, Rumi bursts into sobs.

He doesn't have enough money in his pocket to pay

for a call to weep his heart away. Kumar says that that night, under the full moon, he heard the sound of the dark sea. The sound of love coming of age.

Rumi asks Kumar how much more does he have to grow in order to live with me.

Rising from the picture of the third morning, Su is sleepy. Throughout the day, rain will keep dripping into all the rooms. It'll be evening throughout the day; making room for blankets and books in the middle of all the noises growing louder, Su, asleep, will be visible to me for some time. All manner of children will be moving around inside the house. Whereas, I'm going to need a whole planet to myself to listen to the rustling of trees and the sound of Su's breathing.

Without uttering a word—Su from that room; I from this room—we enter the verandah of the fourth night.

He's already sitting in the blue chair.

In my hand is Marina's book. I've no clue I'll place it in Su's bag when he leaves the day after tomorrow. To keep Marina to myself, this way will be new for me.

Marina—*Love is a flower flooded with blood. You thought it was a chat across the table?*

In the verandah, there's not even the sound of breathing.

Su's glasses are misted over once again. He wipes them with a corner of my scarf.

Is it true that seeds break from a touch?

Only this one line is Miranhshah's. The rest—all of Marina in Su's voice on the fourth night in the verandah.

I came only for five days because you said five days will be enough.

Those five days it would keep raining. Looking for dry corners, right in the middle of smelly children singing and fighting, I would be able to see the misty emptiness left behind by Su, even while he was around, did I know? Just because all those kids were not mine, they would turn out to be all mine, did I know?

The phone would be dead for five days, and Rumi, in his unloved city, sitting in his office, would be weaving Su and I in a way that the venom and sorrow would keep brewing in his eyes. Borrowing money from Aditya, in the middle of the rainy night, he would be looking for a phone booth to grab on to Kumar's voice for a while.

Then, on the last night, sleep comes to us.

Su reminds me this is the last night.

I remembered wrongly that Nastasya Filippovna would rest only after burning the whole wad of a hundred thousand rouble notes. Su is insanely Myshkin. And that too in Marguerite's novel, slipping out of Fyodor's.

I'm trying to weave Su treading impossible paths.

Rumi says all this is happening because I've handed over myself to Marguerite in this way—*the power she has over you, and that one line by Marina. Because Kumar has turned the world into a few sentences for you.* Rumi says the way Su turned up six years ago, and the way he sat across from you quietly…Rumi says he has known it all, since that night, *it has taken you six years to find out.*

Rumi knows the power sentences have, even then he goes on speaking.

After Su leaves, snatching Su's shirt from Tanya's hands I try to look for Su. In the smell of dampness somewhere there is Su's form, but the dampness is soon going to engulf it. Then I'm going to fold it and lower it into the iron box. Only for a little while will it be possible to cover one's face with it and weep.

Having forgotten his white shirt in the story, Su has left it behind in the rear room.

I have no clue. Getting rid of all the children, Tanya sits all day long reading Marguerite. Giving colors to the kids, I want to sit quietly for a while; giving them books, just for a little while. But they keep advancing like a deluge. Looking for dry corners inside, Su has gone outside and is sitting in the rain. Water is pouring down on the temperature of his face.

Su has no clue whose songs are pulling him from some far away platform of the Jahaz Mehal…

On his way to the funeral pyre of someone his own age, Su. From the songs one can't tell anything; the melody is not of lamentation, nor is anyone crying or showing any surprise at Su's presence in their midst. The father of the young man lying on the pyre has to arrange a funeral feast for the whole village of Mandu. *Our crops were washed away by the rains,* he tells Su.

Tanya and I have sat the kids near the pond to clean them up. Uma's black dress is in tatters. Her thin legs are trembling.

Giving to the dead man's father, whatever money he has in his wallet, Su returns to the pond. His face is pale. I look around to see if there's a chai shop somewhere.

All Uma want to do is jump from stone to stone, holding Su's finger.

Blue

To Agneta Pleijel for her novel *Hundstjärnan*

The fragrance of snow, like that of clean glass, is so imperceptible that only a written meditation on it can give any idea of its almost non-existent character.

—Bo Carpelan

One

"I know nothing. I know nothing about the blue in *Blue Eyes Black Hair*. The color I see in your eyes, is it blue?"

"Yes, my eyes are blue."

"I know nothing about blue."

Neither about brown. But, like I don't know about blue, not like that. The relation this has with not writing, not being able to write—that's an old story about my business with blue. But I'm very tired at the moment.

My hair, too, is blue these days. Like some of my books. In the empty air of the street, replicas of blue streaming to me, one after the other.

He is rowing the empty winds with his long arms. The rumor of his presence rises from his wind-blown golden hair and breaks against me. I am blue in the coils of this day. I'll continue to be blue. One day I'll cease to be. Continuing to appear blue even then, I'll cease to be. I breathe only to organize blue. At the very last minute,

I surface from the water to breathe. My hands burn on the stove. I save my arms from turning to ashes.

The rotis I bake are blue. For blue, I battle endlessly with blue weaponry. No one is injured by my assaults. No one believes my blue utterances. They say this is an old story. They can't see my blue, the blue between him and I. I don't want this blue to be visible to anyone.

In this blue, in this invisibility, he weaves me for himself in such a way that I don't have any years, I don't have a form. In this blue, I could be anything from his writer's block to his twelfth century Russian princess sister.

He can't bear the endlessly changing features of my face in his eyes. I flow from the color of his eyes, from the province of his snow, from the despair of his companion. She tells him, you're crazy. She tells him I'm exactly like her. I say, I know. Now, I know. And I won't be afraid. I'll simply dwell in blue. I have no involvement outside of Blue.

Mother was cuddling with father's already dead breath.

He could never show affection while breathing—my father. He used to live in nineteenth century Russia. His home was nowhere else. Because of nineteenth century Russia, he used to visit oceans and snows and sands. Leaning against his home, his lungs would rip. His clothes would tear, his hair would tangle. Talking about this home to anyone, anywhere, he used to turn them into children asking for a story. Then, they would take my father home, rest him and make preparations for his toilet.

They didn't have any love for each other. This is only a phrase, but it's good to watch it carefully. This phrase is about my mother and my father. Now someone will arrive, watch this phrase intently, and the life of this phrase will thrash around. Nothing can be written. Not writing is better. If you write, the eye has to be trained again. And this isn't always possible. A lot of writing becomes like this unwatched phrase—*they didn't have any love for each other.*

I have tried to write blue like this many times, as though this Blue were just a new sentence in my life. It's possible that he's only a new sentence. I've heard that, like every year, I've begun to reside in a new syntax. They just wish some color to be my share again. That I should let a wave of translucence flow across their mirrors. They'll see then, their own reflections, an unfamiliar smile.

They reside in the mirror. They don't descend with me here where there is nothing now but blue. Here, I have to bake rotis with the fire of my blood to be able breathe. Here, I have to light the pyre of my sleep to be able to breathe. Then Blue would recline his long, golden body here for a while. I don't hope this Blue will lie here until I die. This Blue will be seized by some other whim, some other impulse. This Blue will leave me and strike lightning on another roof.

This Blue thinks he'll stay with me in the house of blue, beside a wild brook, across from where a white dome is visible, where we'll separate for just a few moments to seek solitude. Blue writes to me with his eyes blinking on the page. He asks me why I don't stop him from talking about this blue house, why this wave inside him won't calm down.

And I—in a brown house, in a rich brown house, chat up this color brown. This brown is my father's, of my father's temperature, with the eyes of my father. Leaving, my father has sent his eyes for me, hidden in the eyes of Brown. Whatever Brown writes, Brown's eyes perceive the phrase even before he writes it. My Brown's writing doesn't escape this seeing. Today is Blue's night. Inhaling blue, Brown is sitting in the sun, writing. This sun in which Brown is able to sit, open bodied, is the consequence of many days of treeless storms and rain. He tries in his phrases to glimpse the house of blue, where Blue wants me at the moment, and then that white dome which Blue has thrown open for my solitude. Brown opens the body of his phrase like the yawn of a cat. Brown's bones crackle. Brown's body flaps like father's lungs. Brown looks at me like I were his daughter. And then like a beloved. And then like that beloved who now like a daughter he will have to marry off to Blue in a far away land. Growing no end, Brown trickles away through the drain on the roof of our brown house. Brown generates smoke in his blood. Brown nurtures his blood with smoke to commit to the wind. Brown is now in a tomb that his writing has begun to inhabit. Brown has descended into the tomb with my blue. I cry my blue again, in my brown house, in my rich brown house, I plead for blue. Brown shows me smoke, shows me tea, he shows me roti, lulls me to sleep. Seeing father near my writing desk, I cry for father. Then I go to Brown, who is sitting in the sun, and say, stay visible to me, don't stop being visible. Laying my head in his lap, I cry for Blue. Brown says I ask him for a Brown larger than him. His bones crackle. Didn't he know I came to this house to yearn for Blue?

Then Brown is my baby bird in this blue province. He has fallen from the nest. Ants come crawling to this blue patch. This single file is very long. Sitting on the anthills, I chirp. My wings won't be able to lift him. I won't be able to pick him up and put him back in the nest. I chirp in human tongue. I plead for Brown's life with the ants. They keep crawling, as though they hear nothing, just like I hear nothing when crawling in dishes, they are suddenly washed away. Brown is sitting in the sun on the roof, comforting my head with father's fingers. I am in his lap yearning for Blue.

Blue, sitting in our two-day room in the jungle, takes notes. I go inside. There's the lifeless body of a dragonfly under the faucet. I'm afraid to touch it. Then Blue is also there with me. He bends and looks at it with concern. Then touches it with his fingers. Holding it on his index finger, he stands in the filtering sun of the jungle for a long time. There's no hope for life, he's standing. I stand watching from the window. I think this image of Blue will never die in my memory. My memory will begin to live in it. Then Blue will never be gone from me. I go out. He's watching it, as one does a dead thing for the first time. He's wearing a blue garment of some woolen fabric. A few days ago he told me that garment had reindeer forms on it. When I tried to see them again, the reindeer weren't there. He used to always think there were reindeer forms on that garment. He smiled at that thought.

That evening and that whole night were blue. We sat in the cold of the porch, watching the fireflies. He didn't know anything about fireflies, he didn't know what we were seeing that night were fireflies. He thought they were tigers' eyes. I thought if there were that many tigers in this jungle, we would have nothing to fear.

Then I was sad that they were not tigers' eyes. Those fireflies.

Many lands away, in his jungles, on some shore, the moss that the reindeer chews was getting drenched with dewdrops.

Then its wings fluttered open in the sun. It came to on the gentle edges of his fingers. It wasn't in a hurry. It wasn't in a hurry to fly away from Blue into the jungle. Its iridescent wings were testing the complexion of the sun. Under Blue's gaze, it was re-entering its body. I saw father's breath break that night when I had to crawl and sit within mother. The spell in father's eyes drew me towards mother's depth. My house was very blue there, my heart was blue, in the rich ray of a brown, in which I had come to knock at my mother's penury.

In the shadow on page six, I'm not able to glimpse the first three lines on page seven. I'll name this shadow 'Blue'. He'll not be able to drag me out of Brown. He'll turn around and look. He'll forget. I'll turn into a fistful of salt.

Covering his blueness, Blue will begin to cry.

He'll go to the porch and generate smoke from his severed intestine.

Sitting in the night, he'll continue to drink himself.

He'll tell me about the madness of Gustav Fröding.

From the one-time hurt love, he used to visit only women he could pay. Gustav Fröding.

He can't translate Gustav Fröding for me, no one can do it. Fröding is not at all Fröding in any other language. Blue says some sentences to me in his language once again. Perhaps, about Brown. For God's sake, let's be silent for a while.

Two

Just as I can't think about writing in this way. That I pluck a phrase out of Blue's letter and place it on white. And a phrase on white from Blue's letter will have the magic of blue. Blue is not like that.

He is of no use to me. Not even in the ocean sun when he talks to me about my father. We never used to descend into the core. Each word used to fly loose like his golden hair. Each word only a drop from the ocean's iridescent tassel. Also, he never used to swim too far from the shore. Your father is the true story of your life. This sentence uttered by Blue lifts in the moist sunlight of the ocean. I had never heard this sentence, even though it existed, it existed even before I met Blue.

Drinking lemon and tea in the moist sunlight of the ocean, Blue stretched his arms above this sentence and removed my blue scarf.

* * *

This was not possible. I wanted total darkness in my reading of this man called Lawrence. So my mind would stop talking, so I wouldn't turn toward the mirror to learn how to instill the reflected forms of love in my mind. I had to memorize love?

I can lose my memory in Blue. Forget the soft brown stars of his body. Burn my hand cooking rotis. Miss a step coming down a staircase. Cross a road…

I want to believe that it was like this. That this was possible. That words had been extinguished that night. That there was no mirror. That there was no memory of a mirror. That there wasn't love either—that which we begin to call love. There were two trees. Two tall, fragile trees from Blue's country. There was the wind. There was Ingmar's sinking pulse at the crest of the lake, an illusion of a final frame. That night I had no words for that light which was in Ingmar's frame— that which is the light of darkness. It would be possible to see Ingmar like this, how was I to know? In my own country, Ingmar remains unsolved. That madness of Karin. That sudden love between the brother and sister. That which Karin was able to see from the rooftop, in the breeze of her sinking pulse, only she could see. I used to live like a scrap of paper in Karin's darkness. I wasn't Karin, I wasn't

Karin's darkness. That came from Ingmar Bergman's brow.

But this was possible. I was Karin's darkness. There was a scarf over that darkness that had fallen to the floor at Blue's touch.

Two, tall, fragile trees from his country. In the autumn of his country. Their colors turning from yellow to crimson, in the first snow of that season, the first night of snow.

That night there was no love. Two trees were whispering in the breeze. Their leaves, turning from yellow to crimson were touching one another. There was Ingmar's breeze in the light of darkness. Words had extinguished in the head for the whispering of the trees. There was no memory of a mirror. No memory of a body. That night also, perhaps, Blue wasn't there. I hadn't given him blue yet.

Then, that night, too, I had seen the eyes of that wild, ferocious being. Beneath those eyes, my eyes were not human eyes. Human eyes had wearied. That night there wasn't even love.

Blue had told me that we were moving like meteors through his country in those days. The poets of my country. They were not used to being poets in my country. We were not used to being seen as poet meteors. Only Balan knew how, and he too wanted to drown in Ingmar's love. I wasn't used to it, and I had worn my colorful scarves around my neck. It was hard for me to count the scarves, but they were being counted. A blue scarf, caught in rhythm of my share of the fire, was swaying at the apex of the meteor. I used to laugh, and lounging across the stairs of the wooden inn, run toward the laughter of those who were there that night. Where Blue was wrecking himself, I wouldn't stay there long enough so he could say those words to me.

I had seen him just as he had me.

And yet I knew nothing.

I hadn't seen that pitch-black ocean before which he was standing with me, waiting for me. I was always with him, and he, waiting for me before the pitch-black ocean, was turning himself into blue.

Then he climbed the wooden inn, where my laughter was, where the blue scarf was around my neck. He was there till the laughter of all my country's poets died down, when I was descending the wooden inn. His leaves were amber, like the leaves of laurel, like the leaves of his namesake leaves, like the leaves he was named after in his language. His eyes were blue, without a doubt; I was in the shadow of darkness; I was watching them in the shadow of sleep. Then there were his arms, as though it were not possible for me to be elsewhere, as though I couldn't step out of their circle to continue descending the stairs, as though he weren't there, as though his eyes weren't insanely blue eyes, as though my scarf didn't slide off and fall on the stairs…

In my room, in the wooden inn, I'd heard him that night. He used to stay with me and wait for me. He was certain he was with me, and it was me he used to wait for.

I couldn't see him where he said he was.

He touched me, I wasn't there yet. I touched him, I wasn't there yet. I bent down to pick up my scarf from the stairs.

He couldn't believe it. Brown rays had entered my room.

He couldn't believe it. I wasn't able to see blue in the brown rays. He was amber like the leaf he was named after.

He hadn't seen the brown rays in the wooden inn; his eyes were blue.

He didn't know that was to be the night when my mirror would splinter. I wouldn't be able to cross the road visible in this glass. The roti I was baking in this glass would burn to ashes.

I hadn't seen him, before the pitch-black sea, standing beside me.

It wasn't I standing with him before the sea. No one was there. Even he wasn't there. Those days he wasn't writing.

I was only visible when I was in my blue scarf. I wasn't writing.

I used to tell Brown that these days what he was about to write was trembling in the palm of my hand. That I was losing myself in a strange blue, that this blue was of those books for which I used to hide on the terrace of June under a tin sheet. That this blue was of those books that used to sink their poisonous fangs into my mother. She, my mother, had no books. She never used to live in father's nineteenth century Russia. Mother had to save us from death, and this was her daily chore, not like God who had counted out our life-breaths. She had to save father, too, whereas, father was always where Nastasya used to flee from blue to brown to blue. It was not at all necessary to save father. In any case, father used to bury his writing in wooden chests. Who did father write for if not for the termites? Until the telephone broke and scattered, father used to smash it on the floor. Buckets full of the glass of my mother's wedding used to be thrown out of the house like rubbish. We couldn't sleep because of the sound of the sewing machine. Mother would ruin many women's clothes, and I would get beaten like a pickpocket held by the police. I used to weep in Nastasya's blue to Nastasya's brown to Nastasya's blue, and father used to meet me there sometimes. The vase broken by Myshkin's hand used to also be there sometimes. I used to pick up a broken piece to scratch at an itch on my heel. The floral design on that vase was a wave of indigo.

Blue's fingers on my heel are mine. This is not the first night of Blue when there were his fingers on my heel and they were not mine. I had destroyed Blue on the morning after that first night. He was buried on the back seat of the car, and I laughed and cried in the rear view mirror. I was now feeling the cold of Blue's country. Ingmar's lakes and Ingmar's murmuring pines were wrecking the poets of my country. Balan's eyes were red without reason and he was beginning to see his first love in the yellow red maple. After that he would see her everywhere.

Ingmar's frames could appear anytime on the still surface of the lakes. Any tree could turn into a murmur at any moment. There was a lemon moistness of snow in the sunlight in which the funeral processionists of two countries were singing and frolicking in Blue's province when he was trying to meet me in the rear view mirror of his tomb in the back of the car. In his corpse were the corpses of my blue books that had me married to the back seat. The golden locks of his corpse were drifting in my sky. My glass was splintering. In a few moments, an unfamiliar blue line was going to appear between two shards. Then I was going to become Karin's darkness. Karin's darkness was just outside of the seventh circle. Felice, Beatrice, Fanny, Maud, Milena, Sylvia and Marina's bodies were beginning to flow. The sky of Blue's country, the autumn sky of Blue's country was about to turn from pale to black.

They all used to write that darkness—the funeral processionists of Blue's homeland. The darkness that flowed out of the limbs of those seven crossed out females. Agneta used to write it, too. Blue, too, used to write it. Ingmar used to create frames from that darkness, encircling the trees of Blue's country. The murmuring of those trees was the murmuring of Ingmar's frames. Beneath the waveless layers of the lakes were the roots of Ingmar's frames.

Standing in morning's window, drinking the morning, I was trying to avoid the laughter resounding funeral procession for a while. I was unable to decipher Karin's darkness in my limbs. Those people were looking for me from the crack in the door. They were not accepting my refusal. I was breaking and throwing bangles at them through the crack. Then they all acquiesced. Nothing was new for them. However, they had become fearful. Smoking my room with good wishes, they left. They took me with them, so that in my absence I was unable to unlock myself. Despite my absencc, I was traveling with them and laughing with them. I was sitting in my room without myself in the morning window. The window was seven storeys high. I was trying to pry it open with my nails.

I couldn't open the morning window. Brown's radiance was thinning out. It had to be flung open just then.

Then I tried to open it in water. I could open the morning window in water. It was opening in water. In water, the hair falling on my smoldering shoulders burned bright in the mercuric light. Splintering that light, I brought a shard of glass to my wrist. Splintering the light, I bit into it.

Water and mercury were in my mouth. Blue's telephone started ringing. He was not in their procession. He was hiding out in the city in the cluster of his children.

I said I couldn't open the morning window. I didn't tell him it was water, I didn't tell him it was mercury. I was speaking from my drizzling body. Suddenly he began to laugh like his little daughter.

I said this story is now becoming long. I can't escape from it.

He pulled his telephone from the cluster to the snow porch.

Three

Then suddenly the night stars came sparkling into my morning window. Nineteen journeying pairs of feet sounded in the corridor. They halted near my room. Karin's darkness was in the room. Not the brilliance of brown light. I was still sitting without myself, generating smoke in Karin's darkness.

The night stars had appeared and it wasn't night. There wasn't even night's fragrance, night's somnolence. The trees were murmuring in the mercuric light. I was watching the murmur. The hands of my body clock had broken. I couldn't open any glass windows. All the glass windows of Blue's province were sealed shut.

If that was night, then that was the third night. Blue's third night. But Blue wasn't present. That was Blue's third night and I was waiting for the third night. The second night was somewhere else and had eluded me. That night I had almost lost Blue. He was sitting downstairs in the bar, weaving the second night. He was trying to convert it into the second night, when I hadn't even glimpsed it.

The second night was in my room, and I, unaware of it, had fallen asleep. It had watched me. Entering my eyes, it had pushed Blue from the door of the train. In my eyes, he was dressed in my shirt.

I had got up and run to the bar.

He had lost me, and now I was with myself in the smoke and laughter filled bar. His wine had begun to tremble. The other poets had left a space open for me to join them. They had no idea this was Blue's second night, and I had come to the bar to claim that night. This wasn't the day when night stars had appeared in my morning window. This play hadn't opened yet in Blue's country. In the journey this was the town meant for Blue's writing. Here his letters arrived, and here his telephones rang. Here, in this town, later, but still in the midst of the story, a blue letter from my country would continue to fly this way. In this blue letter I would extract Blue's life with brown ink. I would write him a letter in Brown's blood. I'll open his blue eyes and fill them with Brown's weeping. He'll learn to weep blue tears onto the blue of the aerogramme, to not tell me anything, to not talk to me, to not write. He'll learn to burn my hands in my country with his country's fire. He'll learn to sprout night stars in my morning window even from there. He'll learn to hold my sleep hostage in his country. He'll not allow me to see him sitting in the train. He'll not see me crossing the road without him, being slapped by the fat hand of a car on the highways of my country.

This was the second night in Blue's writing town. I had descended into the bar to rescue him. I glimpsed the second night in the blue of his eyes.

That building, in the mercuric lights, was to guide us from the bar to my room. The stairs were covered in blue velvet. And in the stairway mirrors, Blue had taken my hand.

This scene was not mine. There was no dust, no smoke, no fear in searching for night's refuge.

I was dancing well, as though someone had opened up a room for me in appreciation.

He had opened the glass windows of my room—this was Blue's writing town. I couldn't read Blue's writing. We used to talk in a third language and was weary. We never used to weary of not talking. This we were learning in Blue's second night.

There was a telephone that I lifted in the air that night. You know it's this blue fox in my room. He used to see me here even before I came. This Ingmar is no magician. He only encircles the trees. Makes them murmur. In the light of darkness.

This darkness is not the same, not the darkness that we know, you'll have to believe this. This darkness is not that which *you* call darkness. That which I'll not call darkness after I leave here.

I thought the funeral processionists of this country would do exactly what they wrote to us, with dates and times.

Yes, I said, I called them funeral processionists. They are that beautiful. I've heard the sound of their weeping. They're not visible when they weep. They weep in Blue's second night.

And this blue fox, I can't tell you, nor to myself. I know nothing, except that perhaps this is a story. And, perhaps this story is no longer mine.

In this country, all my blue books have snapped open in the light of darkness. Reflected in the waveless layers of the lake, they murmur in the trees.

I hung up the phone in the air.

On Blue's shoulders, on his arms were pictures of faint brown stars in Blue's second night.

Those brown stars on his long back!

Four

"This has no meaning…"

I look at him.

"I write, and yet this has no meaning for me, in this country…"

I don't understand. For me this is a completely unfamiliar sentence.

"No meaning, if you…"

I can't bear that this sentence, fractured in three places, is beginning to breathe.

In the fear of this game, you've quietly slid your writing in my direction. Now it is in my triangular space. I can pick it up and keep it with me. You'll enter my triangle to take it back.

There is a dense ocean in my triangle. There are groves of coconut trees. You won't be able to bear it. I can't bear it. I can't bear the fear of having this triangle fade away.

There's Udayan's house in my triangle.

Brown will weep for Udayan, for Udayan's drowned beloved. Brown will weep as though to write the dense ocean for me to drown in.

Udayan sees himself as a laughing corpse. I'll meet with Udayan in Marguerite and Camus' town. In just a few days, we'll be walking on the banks of the Seine. Udayan and I, on the deluge of yellow leaves. In Marguerite's town, we'll be drinking Marguerite's wine. In Marguerite's rain, under my brown parasol, I'll tell Udayan about Blue. He'll tell me not to upset myself about Brown.

I can't write Udayan the way I write Blue.

In the absence of Vasavadutta, I don't bear Udayan. Sometimes Vasavadutta comes to me. She doesn't know a thing. She thinks the poet of Kausambi never loved her. I try to comfort her. Udayan remains distant from desire. He doesn't know Vasavadutta is alive.

Bereft of Vasavadutta, he has removed himself from the thought of Vasavadutta living.

He says I should step back into blue.

We are all married to one another. Not us; our writing. It's not important to mention names. We all have a derelict home in that town, where on the morning of third December, human beings and animals and birds lay strewn on the roads. The lake of that town was not Ingmar's. That lake had inhaled the poison from the air. It took the lives of its aquatic creatures and saved the lives of a few human beings. I don't tire from coloring Blue in that lake. I called him into that marriage, that congregation.

Blue calls me to that empty house on the banks of Ingmar's lake, where right across is a solitary room. She who is exactly like me will not stay there. Blue doesn't talk to me about her—my twin soul. They are together, so as not to be together in the cluster of their children. She is sitting stiffly in the effort of keeping distant. She wants to write me a letter. A shard of light drops from the cobweb on the spinning wheel in their house. I was looking at the eight copies of Blue's book on the dust shelf at that time. My twin-soul was uncorking red wine for the poets of my country. I had seen that shadow in her eyes. Her straight blond hair fell to her shoulders.

Blue's first night was still two nights away.

My twin-soul had come to the reading where Blue had to read in the music room in the forest. In the candlelight, someone had played the violin and left before it was time.

Of that same night I have the pictures of Blue and my twin soul. I see them in this story, Blue looking my way in the pictures.

Blue's first night was still far away. Sitting with Brown, I try to make out the partial face of my twin. Brown tries, too. He tells me there is this difference between you and your twin. She can't laugh aloud like you.

Five

"He should have let her die while she was yet alive, and wept in her memory."

Brown will weep for Udayan's drowned beloved; he will weep for Udayan.

In Blue's first night, Blue's body was for the sake of my body.

In those seven nights, they didn't meet like Blue's and my bodies.

Two trees whispered in the breeze. Beneath those blue eyes, my eyes were not human eyes.

Blue held the darkness of those seven crossed out females in the autumn of his country.

The pages he wrote were female.

A blue fox. A blue pine. Of seven nights of blue.

Udayan will let him weep. Udayan will let Brown weep in his writing. Udayan is that who'll let him weep without comforting him. Udayan is that who'll laugh until the break of dawn, will make others laugh, until the pyre of the night turns to ashes. We all go in the morning to pick the ashes. We go to Udayan—we laugh and weep—we write and we all gather ashes.

Sometimes Vasavadutta watches him from outside the room. In the morning she too accompanies friends to gather the ashes. Sometimes she too is unaware that Vasavadutta is alive.

Seine is a river. Udayan laughs, arching over the deluge of yellow leaves. This is the city of his poets. This is one of the homes of my Marguerite. She'll continue to write even in her death, so she had said. Only this once will I say her other name. Duras.

Six

In my eyes in Blue's third night, father is on my childhood's roof. I descend the stairs and run onto the street. Father throws a knife at me. It falls in the street. I dodge it and run again. Father throws another knife.

Blue's golden hair is on the white pillow. As I run from father, it catches under me in Blue's third night. He wakes up in the downpour of blades.

Then Brown's father arrived. It was one of Blue's nights. Blue used to lull me to sleep in the sleep of white birds, in the nest of white birds. I used to fly in Blue's circle; he used to watch me fly. My eyes began to flutter with Brown's father. Brown's father pursued me with the honey of his eyes. Then he pulled my scarf off me. My scarf was blue and a child of a scarf. Advancing towards me from the palm of the epic hand that had risen in the palace breeze, it wouldn't keep growing to let me stay draped.

Blue was sitting up. He, too, was wandering, thirsty and lost in strange places, trapped in the whirlpool of many strange people. Brown's father was in my eyes that time when Blue had got up and sewn the white curtains with golden pins.

Even then they all came to take a look at Blue. They all came to my eyes in Blue's seven nights. Babu was also among them, and then, too, that writer of white silk, who had once said he loved me like a daughter.

Babu came—just as my first love—to take a look at Blue. He approached the cot that, like all my other cots, was too small for Blue. I stood under the sheesham tree to make sure Babu did not meet my Blue. I remembered how he had come to meet my Brown.

Babu, full of laughter, like Babu, he was still full of laughter. I looked at him again, and he, holding his blood leg, came toward the cot. Babu's leg was dangling from his knee, and he bent down and held it. Blue was Blue even stretched beyond the cot. There was Blue, and there was his golden hair, and now Babu was looking at it. Where Babu was laughing, under him was his blood—in the grassy soil.

In the presence of Mother Mary, Blue's hands would not separate from each other. I have no idea what he wanted from Mother Mary, what he was mumbling to Mother Mary. In the empty church, I watched him and Mother Mary's soft blue eyes. Once again a shard of light fell from some crack onto Blue's arm. It was leading me away from blue to a likeness of white.

Seven

One seat was assigned to me in that airplane. I didn't grasp a thing. I had woken up in that morning window. Blue was already in the train, having parted from me, and had not let me see him sit in that train. He had stationed me in a café with a mug of coffee and a sugary bun. This is Marguerite's breakfast, he said. I wasn't to see him off at the train. Then that mile long escalator had drowned Blue behind my blind eyes.

I had come out of the café to see the escalator.

In the white costumes, three dancers, kissing their tall accompanying singers, were drowning behind Blue. The girl was wearing a grey sweater. Her face, wet with tears, was a pale face. She was behind the kissing dancers. They were all drowning in Blue's bereavement.

Then there were a lot of dancers from Blue's country who could be seen kissing their singers. And I wouldn't look at them.

Now I was not the most beautiful woman on Blue's planet.

Down below, he was there before the brackish blue of the Baltic, and that most beautiful woman was with him all over again.

Before the brackish blue of the Baltic she was a sentence with a fellow sentence, that was blue, it was blind, and it wept…

***

Aside from the desire to write, this body comes to nothing.

Marguerite's written bodies are nothing but the desire to write.

Then they begin to write and are unable to.

Then they write blue and are sometimes able to.

They can never write Udayan.

Udayan will accept nothing apart from Udayan. I don't have Udayan's flowers, his ashes. Even Udayan doesn't have Udayan's ashes for the laughing corpse of

Udayan. Udayan comes only to drown in books that never surface.

It never surfaced, that book, I couldn't make it surface.

Vasavadutta used to come to me for a while. Then return. Sometimes, she, too, didn't know she was Vasavadutta. She used to come, she used to come asking questions.

She writes blue. She thinks she'll be able to write blue in Blue's bereavement.

Blue will accept anything from her trembling hand, he'll take anything. She sees blue in the cluster of trees, in the glass jars in stores, in the children in the city of London, in the ashes of her books she sees blue. Her hands burn, making blue rotis; she doesn't cross the blue road, is rebuked by the fat hand of a car. Then Krishna came to visit her, he was in despair to see her so overcome with blue. She tried to make Krishna see that blue streak. In Karin's darkness she did not talk words to Krishna. I have only this blue streak, she told Krishna.

This is not I, I am not her who you have come to visit. On the street, she takes Krishna's hand in her own in the fog of Krishna's eyes. This is a hand from her earth, that same earth that was under her feet at one time. There is nothing there except blue now.

Touching the blue streak, Krishna's hand is still Krishna's. She is not able to let go.

Blue will accept anything from the tremors of her writing.

If she asked, will you say your eyes are black? He'd say, yes, my eyes are black.

She asked, do you see the blue fox that I can see? The Lawrence blue? He said I don't know where you take me, but I like it here.

If she asked him, have you seen Nastasya fleeing from Blue to Brown to Blue, like someone with a death wish, he immediately became distressed. He'd say, yes, she can go, whenever she wants to go, she can go. Then he'd get up and change the porch of snow into that of smoke. His body would exhale the fragrance of tears that is the fragrance of his desire from Blue's seven nights.

Blue is childlike; he'll believe anything in the joyful despair of her writing. Like the sound of these words. As though there was some such thing as joyful despair. And for which she had coined a word in her own language: *sudukh*. As though this were the very first word. As though this earth was the offspring of this firstborn word, and now was returning into this word.

Blue scorches his back in the sun of Kovalam's sea. In the sea of Kovalam's night sand, he writes her name—who was there that night.

He lays her on the sand, lays her on top of her name, touches her.

The silver moon on Kovalam's black ocean is now all but copper.

The drops in Kovalam's tassel are now drops of copper.

She is drenched in those drops; she touches him.

And Brown—who comes for a walk on this whiteness.

It is three in the morning and Brown, who just turns up in my eyes for a walk on this whiteness. Groping in his brown cloak, he conjures smoke.

I will say, it's time, we should leave. No?

He'll sit before me and say, that night on Kovalam's black sea…

I'll say yes, that night on Kovalam's black sea.

That very night, later, I had awoken from Blue's sleep and returned to Kovalam's black sea.

My name wasn't there.

There, sniffing at the copper moondrops, were dogs. They were wailing.

Kovalam's lighthouse was revolving like some flaming madman.

Three flaming arms were revolving on Kovalam's black sea.

Kneeling in the sand at that very spot, I wept for Brown. I wept him away from my eyes.

***

Those slums used to make many daughters of my country weep in the name of Bhopal. I asked them—those who came from their beautiful homes to visit the homes of corpses. For many days, many months, many years they came from different places, to play with the children who were slowly going blind in Bhopal.

I had some errands there—just a few errands in Bhopal.

They had called me there to weep in the name of Bhopal.

I held the end of the jump rope in which the children jumped.

I asked the daughters of my land why they came to play with the children who were slowly going blind. I can't remember what their answers were. I remember what I'll say in Bhopal. I come to weep for Brown.

I remember what I'll say in Bhopal. I come fearing blue, to play with the children who are slowly going blind in Bhopal.

I held one end of the rope. They suddenly began to enact the night of second December.

Then they ran into the poisonous night of their play. I, too, fell down in the night of second December.

They said, sister, this is not you who is playfully falling down in the street; it is we. You know nothing. You come here only to weep in the name of Bhopal.

You will only weep for me? Brown says.

She says I know that just by weeping I begin to weep some more. From weeping, I go into the womb of weeping. Then I don't emerge. Not for Blue, not for Brown, not for Udayan, not for Krishna. Do you see this blue streak I have brought back from Blue's land? On that side is Ingmar's lake; in the fire yellow of the maple is the fluttering of my books. This side when you see me, that's not me. I who created me to weep in the name of Bhopal. I who created Brown to weep for Udayan.

All she can do for Brown is weep. On Kovalam's night sand she'll touch Blue. Will sleep on top of her name written by Blue in the sand.

Then on the same sand she wakes from Blue's sleep and weeps for Brown.

Brown says when she weeps—anywhere, or on any sand—when she weeps for Brown, it feels like home.

She says when she weeps for Brown, her weeping for birds and ants also begins to weep. The weeping for termites for whom father used to write. For father who used to write for termites.

Eight

She invokes the body repeatedly. She makes that body journey from father to Brown, stopping in many places on the way. If she asks someone the way, she asks by touching them on the shoulder. She touches the grain that's to be scattered for the peacocks of dusk.

She stops in many places on the way. They hold her back. They are humans and sometimes they desire to hold her back. They forget that she is body. They desire as though she were not body, but a part of a body; some star that fell out of the night. They desire a fallen star.

She asks Vasavadutta the way and passes through the kingdom of Kausambi like a nun. She has heard about Udayan. She remembers something. Holding her body in her own arms, she passes through Kausambi.

She drowns Ganga's seven infants in the Ganga.

Throwing her head back, she laughs. From under the waves, from the bed of seashells, she laughs. From the wrinkle of poison, from the throat of venom.

She doesn't get offended by the desire of humans.

She lets herself be consumed like a fallen star.

Nine

She sees Brown in a picture. He loves her in the picture. One day when she is in Brown's province...she doesn't want to leave. Here she has to meet Brown in numerous chapters.

They live in the picture and then together, in the picture, they touch that grain which is for the birds of the dusk.

The nests of birds fly into their picture. They let them.

The birds pull out straw from the broom lying on the roof of their picture. They let them.

Brown sees her in the picture.

She doesn't want to leave. Here her body doesn't have the fear of blue.

Here her body doesn't have the fear of body.

Then, from somewhere back there it enters the picture. They don't notice it.

She picks up her body from the picture and doesn't say she has to go somewhere.

Brown sees her arise in the picture. Now, she who doesn't have to go anywhere, didn't want to go anywhere, is not with him. She arises and sits up. No one can say whether she is there or she is not there. She picks up her body from the picture. There's someone who leaves the picture in her place. There's someone who can't leave the picture in her place.

When she wakes up in the morning, Brown says this is deception. You have deceived me.

She doesn't think so, but Brown thinks that and by the afternoon, she, too, thinks she has deceived him. Then she begins to weep into the rice on her plate.

In the writing of the dusk, Brown is not able to write the word deception. His hand is like the sky.

The Brown of the dusk transforms himself into the Brown of day. The Brown of day into that of the dusk.

And in this way the surface of this picture trembles, the waters of this picture are churned. This is the way Brown's bones crackle.

Like this, she craves for Blue in the midst of deceiving and not deceiving.

Like this, she picks up her body from the picture. She doesn't want to go anywhere.

Ten

She has brought away Blue's writing from Blue's game. Blue is in her triangle. On the sands of Kovalam's black sea in Blue's seven nights.

Brown packs her luggage for the sands of Kovalam's black sea, for Blue's seven nights.

All the cots in her triangle are too small for Blue. Blue's neck can fall anywhere, severed by the fan circling in her triangle.

When he visits, they all come to my eyes to take a look at Blue in Blue's night.

My mother. Her kin. Her friends and her foes.

That story-teller of mine, made of white silk.

My first Babu.

Brown's father.

My father wielding knives once again.

In my eyes, Blue in Blue's seven nights, is sleeping with his legs folded under him in my maternal grandmother's attic.

I don't know why and how there are so many in-laws, so many neighbors in my grandmother's house.

They peep through the door at the sky-blue clad sleeping form of Blue, at his wet golden hair, at his folded legs.

I try to tell them, no, but they don't listen.

I don't know why they give me silver coins and figs. Why the chickpeas are coated with sugar, why there are strands of red thread in the platter. My clothes are dirty; I am so devoid of the spell he had once cast that I'm afraid Blue will wake up and look at me.

Blue's eyes are not like sleeping eyes. My mother's

brother, like the neighborhood's madman, loudly clearing his scratchy throat, is standing before the attic. My mother's brother *is* the neighborhood's madman. Blue will awaken from this noise, and I'm afraid that as soon as he awakens, he'll ask me where the bathroom is.

Blue comes in through the door of the big house in wet clothes. I get up from the bed. And now, turning around, my mother is on the bed again. She is darning the underclothes I had discarded—fixing their hooks. Behind Blue's back, I glare at her—go away; he will see you, mother of mine.

I pat Blue dry with my long scarf. I lay aside his clothes. Then I pick up my yellow kurta from the bed and help him into it. He lifts his arms to wear my yellow arms.

Eleven

Swallowing the sands of Kovalam's black sea in Blue's seven nights, Brown has withdrawn to the tomb. His heart has swollen in the darkness.

Blue says I should go back.

Blue's four nights remain. I can't get up, he generates smoke, his touch has vanished.

Warangal's farmers are being destroyed; they're putting an end to themselves. They're not farmers of that cotton which is the cotton of wicks in prayer lamps. They are the farmers of the cotton sprayed over with the poison of insects. Swallowing the venom of insects, the farmers of Warangal are being destroyed. We drink lemon and tea in Kovalam's sun. The damsels of Kovalam raise intoxicating eyes to sell colorful scarves. And, as before, on Kovalam's black sea, Kovalam's lighthouse revolves like a madman.

Blue is dissolving in my triangle. Thousands of spirits of his land have come to acquire copper bodies in the sunlight of Kovalam. For some time, just for some time, Blue scorches his back in the sunlight from the sea…

Right after the dance concluded, that dusky girl had followed him. All night they had slept in each other's arms.

That dusky dancer had come to get her after-dance sleep in Blue's arms.

The fear of Blue had developed, and I hadn't brought my body from the picture. Yet.

Then there was the body that I hadn't brought from the picture. That which had accompanied me into Blue's seven nights was not the body of desire. My eyes below those eyes were not the eyes of my body.

He looked carefully at the ring on my hand. I tried to remind him.

They all left, those traveling dancers, and he waited as though that place had slid toward him for someone else. Before the brackish blue of the Baltic, he was with her, waiting for her. Then he was before the black sea with her, looking at her.

He looked at their rings carefully. Those who left. Those traveling dancers.

His father's face had changed into an infant's before it had silenced.

In the forest of Periyar, watching the fireflies, Blue remembered him. He wasn't conscious. He was watching him walk in that translucent body from one age to the other.

Then he had thought they were tiger's eyes, those fireflies. All those fireflies.

Twelve

His tears don't fall when he's alone. Brown weeps leaning on Udayan's tears. Fallen tears from an earlier time are already in the soil. Brown is afraid to weep alone.

Even then his tears don't fall where there are traces of Udayan's tears.

We try to weep even in space. There are some traces of tears even in space. The traces of tears of falling stars. Of angels, who, delivering messages, hide from God and weep. The tears of darknesses between stars that do not fall with the falling stars. The tears of those mirrors that are pure, devoid of reflections, and in whose depths the dazzling beloveds have drowned. The tears of that effort we make in this story and are unable to.

In this story, the one who has been left behind is always Brown. In this story many characters like this transform into Brown. Vision always limits to see Brown. Heart always seethes to contain him. No one can dye them—brown eyes are that deep they live in this world like drowned eyes. Like a smashed child, Brown falls from the nest. Ants always come toward him. Brown knits brown phrases that termites listen to. Brown laughs, laughs loudly, even then his laughter can't be heard. When he weeps, Udayan hears him, or Udayan can hear him. Udayan tells him the story of a fruit in Blue's seven nights. Just some one fruit falls into the scoop of the hand. There's a swamp beneath the trees. One has to hold the fruit that falls into the scoop of the hand. The rest are swamp fruit.

In space there are traces of Blue's tears, too. The tear-traces of that place where she's with Blue on the banks of the black sea. Before reaching there, she traces her footprints in the sand on Blue's left. She doesn't know when she'll rise from the picture and go there where Blue touches her, waits for her even after she arrives. She lifts her body from the picture and is unable to do so. She weeps for Brown even there where she has to go, where she is, and she hasn't reached yet. She doesn't know who she is addressing and when, what room she is in. She doesn't know why Brown's mother, Brown's father have entered Brown's eyes to take him there where they have gone. Fearfully, Brown approaches her bed. She opens her eyes for Blue where Brown, in fear of his ancestors, is snuggled against her, trying to sleep. She gathers Brown and closes her eyes that are moist for Brown and craving for Blue. Blue's golden hair shines in the void of the room's darkness.

They always call us to them these days. Father, from my childhood's roof, throws knives at me. They want to take us far away from this fear. They want to take us with them to alleviate their own fear. They want to take us with them revealing their fear.

I'm on the black ocean right there where my footprints are. The wind is blowing. Blue is not there. His footprints have been washed away by the tide. I touch myself. The wind grows stronger. Instead of high waves, many white sheets rise and come toward me. Blue will be behind them, I think. The sheets come toward me. I draw back, where my footprints were, my feet are now not there. The wind is very strong.

The black ocean calls me loudly to cover me with white sheets.

I try to run toward the sea and away from the sea at the same time.

Thirteen

This is Blue's second night in Blue's writing town. Blue has to interrupt the second night in the middle and go somewhere. We try to cross the road from the door of the inn. Across the road, on the bank of Lake Vannern, there is a statue of a waitress. At this hour of the night, the waitress is clad in a coppery green. Her age in this green is nineteen. The moon's reflection on the waves in Lake Vannern trembles over her.

Before Blue's second night began, Blue and I met him who had placed his mourning in green on the bank of Lake Vannern.

I have to be the world's most beautiful woman, the most graceful dancer, the most enticing traveler. In the wooden inn, in Blue's first night, at Blue's saying, I have to be. The beauty that is his alone, for which he is here in the shape of blue to illumine traveling dancers, at this moment, in this inn, in the dark land of Ingmar's waveless lakes. In the light of darkness this beauty is for me and I have to assume it. Suddenly this is too much for me, a labor greater than my weariness. I try in this story, but it wouldn't listen to me. The sound of Blue's feet on the wooden steps begins to approach me. I can't write this.

Brown will not say anything that I must accept.

My traveler scarves are not for Brown.

The intoxicating colors of those scarves are not to color my eyes when I'm in Brown's eyes.

I show him the pain of my blue teeth, from which every morning a few drops of blood pour out. On my arm, my lip, I show him the sting of the bee. With the hard nails of his toes, he scratches my foot where warm ants have bitten me and left for their homes.

Are my teeth about to fall? I ask him. He says, that's possible.

Blue shows me that lonely house on the banks of Ingmar's lake, across from which is that solitary room.

He spreads a mat for me in that lonesome kitchen, arranges some cups in the place of other cups, some books in the place of other books.

He sends me pictures in which I'm the most enticing traveler in the world in the sun of Kovalam's sea, the most graceful dancer.

Around my neck, on my shoulders, on my arms, in my hair, are colorful scarves. In my eyes is Blue's reflection that, drenched with perspiration, pulls me into the picture.

There's someone there who, before entering the inn in the morning, looks at the green statue on the banks of Vannern.

Watching over the banquet table of twenty funeral processionists, he raises his eyes to look at the banks of Vannern.

Every night, on his way home from the inn, he looks at it in the northern light.

In blue's second night, Blue had to go somewhere. He was forgetting that story somewhere. How did that girl die?

That girl's hair was dripping wet in the stone statue.

Acknowledgements

As always, my companion Rustam Singh's patient reading of the manuscript with the experienced eye of an editor was immensely helpful. However, I take responsibility for errors that might still be in there.

Also, I thank him for creating all the solitude in our shared work space that a work in progress inevitably requires. More often than not he *is* that solitude.

Let me also observe that when the time came for my friend Meena Arora Nayak to reread the original texts, she found that she was beginning to translate them.

I'm extremely grateful to artists Sandeep Singh and Mandeep Singh Manu whose labor of love shows in the beauty of the book you have in your hands.

I'm also grateful to Kamila Junik, the Polish translator and fellow explorer of *Blue* for letting me use her writing so generously.

— Teji Grover

Blue is nothing but for that passion. Rather it's a color on account of that passion. A perspective which is not aware what it's a perspective of—in other words the "passion" of which it's a perspective is itself the "cause" of it. Otherwise blue is nothing, not even a color. "Blue" seduces. You feel there's something beyond it, on the other side of it—a certain hue, a form, a three-dimensional entity, but however high you're able to fly, "blue" continues to stretch beyond you. It's the color of not-being which can be glimpsed only from the distance of "passion". For those who are under the illusion that writing requires things other than words, reading *Blue* is a must; those who think words are not part of those other things. But *Blue* must also be read by those who are not under that illusion or who are under the illusion that they're not under that illusion.

You, Teji, *you* must read *Blue*. You should see the inverted form of your own "passion".

How I wish I could read *Blue* standing in your place!

— Madan Soni's letter to the author